THE FOUR OF US

by

A. M. Keen

Copyright © 2023 A. M. Keen

ISBN: 9798399490229

All rights reserved.

The right of A. M. Keen to be identified as the author of this work has been asserted by him.

This is a work of fiction. Names, characters, places, incidents, and dialogues are the products of the author's imagination or are used fictitiously.

Where locations are used, all characters described herein are fictitious. Any resemblance to actual people, living or dead, events or locales is entirely coincidental.

OTHER BOOKS by A. M. Keen

Drawing Down the Moon (formerly Witch)
Tales of Averon: The Dark Army
Tales of Averon: The Beast
Tales of Averon: Dawn of the Great War
The Midnight Inferno
The Long Walk Home
World's Apart (co-author)

My story. My confession.

- Callum Clark. October 2018

Chapter 1: The Wolf Pack

When you're a kid, everyone delights in telling you that your childhood years are the best of your life. At the time you think they're all full of shit. You have to get out of bed every morning and roll yourself into school, spending at least 6 hours a day learning things you're never going to need again once you graduate, and spend the entirety of the day surrounded by absolute morons you're supposed to call your peers. One of the most idiotic things about school is just how excited the teacher's become when presenting to you how x equals y on a faded black board. So faded, in fact, that it appears grey once they begin scrawling equations in chalk across its surface. And, so old, you can see where a kid from years past used a pen to write *'Tennant is a wiener,'* knowing full well it would never be removed in its entirety.

At home you're badgered by parents, forced to eat vegetables and other foods you don't like because otherwise you run the risk of enraging the hand that feeds you, and being sent to bed with an empty stomach.

However, as you get older and spread your wings into the real world, you realise that life isn't as great as you thought it'd be. You're not going to be the next John Wayne, you're actually going to lug heavy goods around in a warehouse for eight hours straight, possibly longer if an unexpected bill lands on your doormat. You sit behind a desk crunching numbers for a guy that can't be bothered to do it himself, or find your anxiety raise at the beginning of a shift, dreading the next eight hours that are about to commence. That's when you pine for the old days. The days when a bill was something you got on a birthday, when you had nothing to pay for and your biggest worry was handing in your book review homework for Mrs Hodgett which you'd left until the last minute.

This type of homework I didn't mind doing. Every other kid in my class reviewed the basic novels such as *Treasure Island*, *Alice in Wonderland* or some other literary classic that cemented itself a place in history. Not me, though. I remember my parents being called into school by said Mrs Hodgett because I'd chosen to review Robert Bloch's 1959 novel, *Psycho*. I didn't see anything wrong regaling my fellow 14 year-old students of Norman Bates' misdemeanours at the Bates Motel, but I guess most other 14 year-olds were not ready for that, especially when I began to explain the real life case of Ed Gein who inspired the story.

Yep, that got me in a meeting with the principle, Mrs Hodgett and my parents. That became the first sign that I'd grow to love horror, and in particular the old universal monster movies that would play out on television over the weekends late at night.

I have many, many fond memories which I recall from my childhood, and everyone who told me these were the best years of my life were indeed correct.

I also believe that your childhood is affected by those around you, and not only were my parents supportive of me and my wishes, but my friends were, too.

It's impossible to look upon your childhood without recalling your friends. Not the ones you saw at school and took a lesson with here and there, but those you sought out. Those you sat with at recess and walked home with. Those who came to your house and slept over. Those you saw for entire weekends, exploring the woods, building dens and just hanging out with.

I was lucky enough to have a group of friends like this, and I swear to God that no friends I had since were as good to me as those three kids.

Chris Lester, Charlie Beaumont, Louis Johnson and I were pretty much inseparable throughout our school years. We argued, of course, and fell out on many occasions, but it never lasted long. We stood together as unit. You messed with one of us, you messed with all of us. It didn't matter what had happened or what the odds were, we stood together and never backed down.

As a collective, we called ourselves The Wolf Pack. Now, this was years before that phrase became cool and trendy with the wrestling kids. Its name reflected our brotherhood and bond, so to speak, and something I took great pride in being part of. We coined the name from our behaviour. I don't even know when it started, but we began howling like wolves whenever something good happened, or just when we were happy. It was nothing more than a quirk, but it separated us from everyone else.

Of course, we never did any of that shit when people were around, we didn't want to gain the reputation as dorks amongst our peers. We were a grade or so above that in our schools social standing, and trust me, that was hard enough to maintain every day we attended school. We kept The Wolf Pack name to ourselves, but our bond as friends was never hidden.

This could often paint us with a bullseye at school, in particular from the generic, red-headed jock Troy Peller and his best friend Billy Brewster. These two older kids would often seek us out and mess with us. Sometimes with their fists as well as their words, but they could never break us down. I think that was why we became targets to them. They couldn't break our spirit, and that pissed them off. But, I'll talk more about them later.

Chapter 2: Setting The Scene

The reason I'm writing this account is to help put to bed the biggest skeleton in my closet. I've kept this hidden away during my lifetime. Now, as a father and grandfather, and with an illness that's going to send me to the pearly gates sooner rather than later, I have to break the promise I made one cold, wet October afternoon back in 1968. My friends and I committed something so horrendous and vile that day I thought for sure we'd spend the rest of our lives behind bars. We dodged a whole heap of bullets fired toward us, too. Any other time, any other place we'd have been caught, of that I have no doubt. There were one or two people I believe figured it out. One for sure, because he told me so himself. Lady luck shone down upon us, and through everything we remained outside and above the law.

    To my friends; I'm sorry. I'm sorry to bring your names to attention. I've carried this around for over fifty years, as have you. I need to make my peace, and this is the only way I can do it. I have to, for my own sake.

    For you to understand what happened to my friends and I back during that fall, first you have to know a little bit about the world and what was happening in America during 1968.

    Vietnam raged across the oceans. North Vietnamese communists launched the Tet Offensive. 15,000 Latino high school students in Los Angeles walked out of their classes to demand a better education. The great Martin Luther King was assassinated on the balcony of the Lorraine Hotel. Andy Warhol became critically injured in a shooting because he lost a copy of a play. Arthur Ashe won the US open. Boeing released the 747. Tommie Smith and John Carlos raised their fists on the Olympic podium to protest violence and poverty toward African Americans. And, of course, Nixon won the presidency by just 0.7 per cent of the votes.

I was 14 years old at the time, and too engaged in other interests such as Bonanza, The Beverly Hillbillies and Mission Impossible to notice the world events taking place around me. As a teen I enjoyed reading comic books and drawing my own super heroes. I think it would be safe to say that I existed in a world of my own. I had a bubble of simple life interests and nothing affected me, either in a positive or negative way.

We lived in Millers Fall, a rural town located between Ellport and Portersville. Self-contained, with its own police force, fire department and schools. The nearest hospital could be found in Butler. To me, it was the greatest place in the world to live, and looking back, the greatest place in the world to grow up.

Chapter 3: Charlie Beaumont

My story began one morning on a day no different to any other in Millers Fall. I woke up, washed, brushed my teeth, dressed, went downstairs and had my breakfast whilst Dad read the paper. WISR played on the radio in the background, ignored by my father as he scoured the morning pages to see what was what in the world. He looked up and greeted me as I took my seat at the varnished table, its surface kept pristine by my ever-cleaning mother. She pottered around as usual, making lunches, topping up drinks, the usual housewife stuff that existed back during that time period.

I chowed down on the many slices of toast Mom had served before saying my goodbyes and leaving with my books, and sometimes a book review for Mrs Hodgett. God bless her.

The thing I love about autumn is the suspended reality it seems to harbour. Warm at times, but not as warm as those long, summer days you've just endured. Chilly, but not as cold as the oncoming winter that would take hold in a few months' time. Autumn acted like the erratic clown at a traditional travelling circus, the one who comes out with buckets in each hand. In one bucket confetti waited to be launched high into the air, flittering upon the audience in a plethora of vibrant colours.

The other contained water, and you just hoped to God he launched it as far from you as possible. Sometimes Autumn threw a pleasant, late summer day that made you thankful it hadn't produced a rain, a gale or both. You could look at other towns and cities in the area and see from reports that they suffered storms and rain, and like an audience member at that circus, you looked on, thankful that it hit them and not you. Other times, well... you just had to suck it up and realise today it's your turn to get the water. The clown always got you, sooner or later.

I loved the unpredictability of the season, but found myself longing for those warm, golden days of the late summer months. If mother nature had put me in charge while she took a few days off, that's all we'd be getting. Later summer for all of us.

I stepped out into one such morning sometime in early October. Golden beams of sunshine almost tricked me into thinking summer had returned, but, of course, it hadn't. A gentle, cold breeze chipped away at my coat. My satchel hung heavy as I marched along the sidewalk and headed toward the park.

Out of the four of us, my friends and me, I happened to live farthest from school, and the only kid who lived on my daily route was Charlie. Charlie Beaumont, the wise ass, take-no-shit kid who had no fear of anyone or anything. One confident son of a bitch. His dad had been something of a boxer back in the day, entering tough man contests before trying his hand in the amateurs. That rubbed off on Charlie, as the pair often trained in their yard together, his dad offering help and advice on becoming the next Mohammed Ali. Since domestication had entered his dad's life when Charlie's older sister, Edith, had been born, the professional boxing stopped, but he always trained, and trained with his son.

Charlie himself had no interest in boxing for money or taking it on professionally. It was something he did with his dad, and just something he loved doing. The only problem is, sometimes you get caught inside a bubble of confidence that may not reflect the truth of the outside world. As hard as Charlie trained, there were still a few kids at school that had his number.

Charlie's confidence got him into trouble with the likes of Troy Peller and Billy Brewster, the jock and his friend who terrorised kids of all ages, and without discrimination. Those two assholes often targeted Charlie, but our other friend Chris, too. In all honesty, Louis and I took shit from the other kids by means of association, so the four of us attended school every day with the knowledge that one of us at least would have a run in with the dastardly pair. Still, this didn't deter us, and it certainly did not deter Charlie, who itched to get into a fist fight with Troy Peller just to see how much of a boxer he had become.

Charlie took shit from no one, including adults he thought had wronged him. You could often find him arguing with teachers about his grades, getting into trouble and swearing blind it wasn't him, that kind of thing. Hell, Mrs Beaumont attended that many meetings with the principle that a chair had been etched with her name on it. I joke, of course, but he was the kid that had mischief written all over him. Always up to something during school hours, but never doing anything that warranted suspension or worse.

In general, Charlie was a happy kid, but if you did anything he didn't agree with, like the time when Mr McGruder at the convenience store short changed him for a soda he brought, well, Charlie had a wonderful talent for causing a scene and putting you in your place so that everyone knew you'd done wrong. After that particular outburst toward Mr McGruder, Charlie had gotten himself and his family banned which caused two things; the first, a real headache for his poor parents. They had to go out of town for the simplest of items, which back in those days was a huge deal. They never mastered the art of buying everything they needed in one shop which only fuelled their disdain.

The second? Charlie became more intent than ever to cause the store owner hassle. If we happened to be together and called in for anything, Charlie would obey the rules and stand outside, as requested. However, Charlie liked to stand at the store front and announce to any customers going in that he'd been banned. Not because of any poor behaviour or malicious intent, but because Mr McGruder short changed his customers, and he'd been the one to catch him. This in turn prompted the customers to challenge the poor old shop keeper about his actions.

If this wasn't enough, Charlie also liked to pretend he'd seen a rat scurrying around the shelves whilst inside purchasing some candy, always in earshot of someone about to enter. After months of Charlie's mischievousness the old, balding shopkeeper gave in and lifted the ban on Charlie and his parents. Not because he felt that Charlie had learned his lesson, but instead to stop the reputation he was beginning to gain around town.

Whatever the circumstances he faced, Charlie stood tall with the best of them. I'm telling you this now, as you'll soon see how important a role he played in this whole shit-show we became involved in.

I approached Murphy's Park, a huge green area in the centre of town and noticed my friend perched on the usual wooden bench waiting for me to arrive. Even though he faced away from me, his scruffy, brown hair and green combat jacket were dead giveaways. The Vietnam war continued at its height across the oceans, and I always believed that Charlie wore the jacket to show solidarity with all of our armed forces fighting there. If he'd been allowed, he'd have volunteered to be drafted himself, firing guns, throwing grenades, screaming at the top of his voice, and, knowing Charlie, loving every second of it.

Across the green, in the distance I noticed a bunch of other kids also making their way to school. I could see the drug store, the bakery and Ted's Barbers. I worked Saturday's at Ted's. Not cutting hair, just sweeping it from the shiny, varnished floor and giving the place a general tidy around. Listening to the old timers chatting and put the world to right made me smile, and I enjoyed it, even if I was just a simple dog's body scurrying around with a tattered sweeping brush.

"Hey douche," Charlie shouted as I came into earshot. He'd noticed me.

"Ass clown."

Charlie smiled and ambled up beside me. "Anything good happen last night?"

I shook my head. "Nah. Watched TV, did some drawing, that's about it."

"Me either. God it's so boring when summer ends."

"Why don't you try something new? Like reading, or listening to music or something?"

Charlie smirked. "You mean like you? Read comics and stuff? Nah, it's not me. We have too much of that crap at school."

"What about music? Got any favourite bands? The Beatles are pretty popular at the moment."

"I hear it all the time. Got mom's radio blaring downstairs, Enid's record player blaring upstairs. At the moment I hate music. I'd rather sit and listen to my grandpa curl out a brown loaf."

"What the hell?" I giggled. Charlie smiled back.

"Well, you stop by and spend an entire day listening to The Monkees and Elvis. Man, anything sounds better than that trash."

"Why didn't you come over to mine? We could have done something better than that."

Charlie's smiled subsided. He groaned. "I got grounded."

"What'd you do this time?"

"I got into an argument with Edith and called her a whore."

I laughed. Only Charlie would blurt something like that to a family member.

"She's gonna kill you one day, you know that?"

"I'd have been fine but mom was standing behind me. She'd heard the shouting over the music and came up to see why we were arguing. Yep, she heard it straight from the horse's mouth."

Sometimes I could empathise with the rest of the Beaumont family. They had to live with Charlie, and that couldn't be easy.

"If you were that bored, and grounded, why didn't you do your homework?" I asked, being a smart-ass.

Charlie stopped, frowning with disgust. "The hell are you talking about, Cal? Homework? Really?"

I shrugged. "It was just a suggestion."

"I'll never be bored enough to do my homework. Never in my life. Ever."

We reached the end of the park and crossed the road, not needing to stop for traffic. "Speaking of homework, did you get the math done?" I said as we hopped the kerb and continued our journey.

"Shit!" Charlie jumped and clenched his fists. "I knew there was something."

"You're in it deep this time," I said with a smile on my face. "Mrs Scott is going tear you a new one."

Mrs Scott and Charlie had a, well, strained relationship you could say. Charlie never went out of his way to wind her up, but he caused her so many issues. Never doing homework was one, holding his hand up and saying he 'didn't get it' being another. If Charlie didn't understand the math he just didn't do it. As much as Mrs Scott would encourage him, once the light was off nobody was home. And in Charlie's case, they wouldn't be back for a long, long time.

A huge, devilish grin engulfed my friend's face. "Cal, Mrs Scott is a young, hot-blooded woman, and I am a seasoned expert when it comes to members of the fairer sex. In fact, I have an unofficial PhD when it comes to women."

"And an official PhD in bullshit."

Mrs Scott didn't appear attractive to me, not like Miss Wincott with her long, red hair, but she was young, and a few guys were sweet on her.

"Cal, you underestimate my skills," he began, placing an arm around me. "You watch. I'll sweep her from her feet." He swiped an open palm across the sky. "I'll make her feel so special that giving me detention will be the last thing on her mind."

"If you come out of the classroom with an extension to do your homework I'll be impressed."

"My friend, that will be the least I'm getting from her. I'll get a peck on the cheek from her as I leave today, just you see."

Millers Fall High School. An establishment as bland and plain as its name might suggest. Long, tiled corridors with lockers either side stretched into the distance, baring a whole heap of generic classrooms and an empty trophy cabinet hidden from view somewhere near the principal's office. America the beautiful. I guess it did its job. It hadn't been closed down, so something was going well.

We hadn't been there long, my friends and I, having made the move from Cameron Drake Junior High just the month before. I transitioned quite easily, as we all did. No drama, no anxiety, just four average kids moving to another average school.

I opened my locker and placed a few belongings inside. The odour of sweaty feet enveloped my nostrils, reminding me to take home the socks I'd thrown in there last week and forgotten about. I took a hold of my fragrant geography book and placed it into my bag. A few feet away the goddess of our school, Erika Ricketts, stood chatting away to her best friend Stacey Shawcross. Erika, with her long blonde hair, piercing blue eyes and immense beauty melted my heart.

If ever a picture of perfection should be created, Erica was that picture. Stacey, the leggy brunette was also pleasing on the eye, but Erika was the standard bearer. I never believed her beauty could ever be matched. That was, of course, until the day my daughter was born. But, back in 1968 as a hormonal teenager, I only had eyes for this siren. She was off the market, of course, as most girls who bare immense beauty tend to be. Rumour had it her boyfriend came from out of town and happened to be a member of The Pagan's motorcycle gang. The fact that he picked her up from school in a pickup lead me to believe this was, in fact, bullshit.

The two beauties chatted away to themselves, blissfully unaware that I even shared the same corridor as them both. I eavesdropped a little on their conversation, picking out various words and phrases, but couldn't quite hear what they were saying. At least, that was until Charlie entered the conversation.

"Good morning ladies," he began, resting against the lockers like the coolest cat intown.

"What do you want?" Erika snapped. Charlie had decided a few months back that he would attempt to take her on a date. This was rebuffed of course, in the sternest of fashions. That hadn't deterred him, though, but the longer he tried, the more frustrated she became. This delighted Charlie, and he'd turned it into a wind up ever since.

"Erika, now that you're my girlfriend, I want you to know I'll support you anyhow I can."

"I'm not your damn girlfriend!"

"Why don't you just leave her alone?" Stacey blasted, entering the conversation without an invite.

"Stacey, why the jealousy? I've told you that if Erica and I split up, then you get your chance. You just need to wait."

"You are such an asshole," Erika whittled. The two girls walked away.

"Erika!" he shouted.

"What?!"

"Remember, I booked us a table at Federico's tonight. 7pm. Only problem is I couldn't afford it. You okay picking up the tab?"

"Fuck off, Charlie!"

The girls stormed away.

"Is that you using your charm?" I asked as I closed my locker.

He smiled. "No, that was just the warm up. It's the *Beaumont* Charm that reels them in."

We stood outside Mrs Scott's room as the bell rang. Kids began shuffling past us to enter their classes on time.

"This is the real deal, Cal my boy. Watch and learn, buddy, watch and learn." Charlie made his way into the classroom. Mrs Scott stood at her table, arranging some papers into an acceptable pile. "Good morning Mrs Scott, it certainly is chilly outside this morning. I have to say, you look simply ravishing."

To this day I look back on Charlie as a subdued genius who could have succeeded in anything he put his mind to. He loved to fool around, was a tad eccentric in my opinion, but as a friend none could be more loyal.

Chapter 4: Arranging A Camp Out

Lunch. The biggest free for all in school history. Survival of the fittest, the weak will fall, of that there is no doubt. If you happened to be late out of class and heading to the dining hall, then say your prayers. Finding a seat became a competitive bout of musical chairs, where insults were hurled toward the victor instead of praise. Looking back on it, they should have made competitive seat finding a sport. Man, today's UFC would have nothing on a bunch of high school kids fighting for a chair back in '68.

Teachers patrolled the cafeteria like wardens patrolling recess inside a prison. I was one of those kids who just so happened to be late leaving geography this particular lunchtime, thanks to that god-damned fart knocker George King. George had decided in his idiocy to prank Mr Bassford during our lesson by hiding his chalk. Of course, all hell broke loose when he couldn't draw a basic US map to show us where fault lines ran, which resulted in all of us being kept behind until somebody squealed. The piggy just happened to be my main squeeze, Erika Ricketts. To be fair, though, she lasted ten minutes in an attempt to preserve George's anonymity, but I guess even a beautiful blonde has to eat at some point?

I entered the chaos a few minutes later and scoured every inch of the battlefield for my friends. I could see nothing familiar in the mass of bodies. A plethora of various coloured garments bustled before my eyes, back and forth. In between each I could see nothing except for more bodies and more colour. My senses became overloaded. I swear to God that was my first experience of a bad trip. A hand rose above the madness and waved. "Cal!" My focus drew upon Louis, standing above the crowd, waving toward me like someone lost at sea.

"Mr Johnson, sit down!" boomed Mr Toms of the science faculty. Louis shit a brick and sat down in an instant.

I pushed my way through the bodies and found my buddies sitting at a table. They'd saved me a chair. God knows how. Battered them away with a stick, maybe? I didn't ask. I dared not.

"How you doing, man?" Chris asked as I perched my butt beside him.

"God damn George King. Farting about in class so bad that Mr Bassford kept us back."

"I hate Bass-ass," Louis replied. "I hate George King too, come to think of it."

Louis could be something of a worrier when the need arose. He hated trouble and was deathly afraid of his father, who had a reputation as a staunch disciplinarian. Don't get me wrong, Mr Johnson was a great guy, and Louis could pretty much do whatever he wanted, but there were rules. In by nightfall during summer. Do your chores. Don't lie. If Louis got in trouble, his ass had an appointment with a leather belt. Because of that, Louis always tried his best to keep on the straight and narrow. But, this lead to something of a nervous disposition. Louis needed a lot of encouragement when we were together, as his fear of a repercussion outweighed his sense of adventure. Even if we decided to spend time down at the park of an evening. During summer he left a whole lot sooner than he needed to, and in winter he just didn't bother at all.

"No one likes Bassford," Charlie said, preparing to take a bite from his meal.

"So, Cal, what did Charlie get detention for? He won't tell us," Chris asked me.

I snorted. "You haven't heard?"

"No? What did he do?" Louis enquired.

Charlie shoved a spoon full of mashed potato into his mouth and smiled. "A legend never tells his own stories," he said, his voice muffled by his meal.

I removed my sandwiches from my bag and placed them on the table. "He proposed. To Mrs Scott."

"He did what?" Chris squealed. He had a high pitched, almost pre-pubescent laugh. It was something that generated humour itself, like a chuckling tommy gun or something of that nature. Often we found ourselves laughing at Chris' laugh, and forgetting what amused us all in the first place.

"Honest. He went to the front of the class, got down on one knee and proposed. It was the greatest thing I ever saw. Mrs Scott went bright red."

Louis chuckled. "That's amazing."

Charlie smiled. "Well, it got me out of math as I spent the rest of the lesson in the corridor. But you know something, Cal?" he said, looking across the table to me.

I unwrapped the rest of my lunch. "What?"

He smirked. "She never said a damn thing about me not doing my homework."

"Look what we have here," came a voice through the mass of sound. Troy Peller and his shadow Billy Brewster approached our table. Troy, the big, red-headed athlete had been the bane of our collected lives since we arrived as freshmen, but he often singled out Chris, purely because of his background. Chris' dad had been drafted to Vietnam, something both he and his mother had taken very hard. Before that everything had been fine. Dawn, Chris' mom, had been a wonderful person, always spritely, always smiling, but the fact that her husband vanished during service had been enough for her to slump into a depression.

It fell on Chris to care for her instead, as she could not shake the weight of losing her husband. She never left the house, so God knows how the bills got paid. The house itself had started to fall into disrepair. When you visited Chris at home you walked along a garden path where long grass spilled over from the lawn. Inside was no better. Mould appeared in most rooms. They were tidy and unclean, with a stale, sweaty smell that wafted through the entire residence.

All of this became common knowledge to the people of Millers Fall. Troy Peller, only two years our senior, often insinuated that Dawn paid the bills by being a hooker, and that he'd screwed her multiple times. Peller was also captain of the wrestling team, which meant his ego had become as big as his biceps. That tells you how much of a specimen he was. Not even the oldest kid in school, but cemented there as it's alpha male.

"Screw you, redwood," Chris replied, avoiding eye contact with the wrestling team captain.

"You know, Lester, it must be really hard for you. Your dad is missing in Vietnam, probably dead. He went over there wanting to die, I bet. I mean, if I had a son like you I'd be so disappointed. He wanted to die to get away from you. And your mom? Well, she's so strapped for cash we all go to your house and fuck her for a couple of cents."

Chris stood. "Fuck you! Come on, you want to fight me?" He launched toward Troy. Both Charlie and I restrained him. He was slippery, though, like a freshwater eel.

"Don't listen, Chris, he ain't worth it. Everyone knows his dad's a pussy and ran away from service," Charlie said, stoking the fire.

Peller snorted. "What'd you say, asshole?"

"We all know you pretend to be tough because your family are pussies."

Before we knew it a shoving match erupted. I pushed a few times, but who I shoved I have no idea. Mr Toms appeared and pushed Troy away from our table.

"Okay boys, break it up."

After a few moments of shouting, cooler heads prevailed and we managed to return ourselves to the mild mannered fourteen year-old's we'd been just a few moments before. Troy took his leave, but not before flipping Chris the bird.

"He's such an asshole," Louis stated. Louis, the ever present but ever petrified of anything happening, had done little to calm the situation.

Chris snarled. "I'll kick his ass if he says anything like that again."

To be honest, we all felt the anxiety Chris suffered over the Vietnam war. My Dad had done a tour, as had Louis' and Charlie's. My Dad hadn't changed so much on his return. He'd seen shit, I knew that much, but he never exaggerated to me what it was. Often I would catch him sitting alone in the evening, his eyes glazed and unflinching. Those were the times I knew he'd be remembering what happened out there. I swear that if you looked hard enough you could see his memories playing out in the eyes themselves, like a mini film projector presenting images he'd pushed to the deepest, darkest recess of his mind.

Even later in life, I would ask him what happened during his tour, and he'd just smile and say "most of the guys out there had it worse than what I did." Dad went to his grave without a single mention of what he'd done or seen during Vietnam, not even to Mom. Sometime I wonder if that affected her. You know, that he kept something secret? That a period of his life was just non-existent and hidden away from everyone. In any other situation this would be a cause for concern, but when someone returns home from serving their country in war, people are more understanding if you refuse to talk about it. At least, Mom was, but I think it chipped away in the back of her mind that he wouldn't share anything about his experience with her.

Charlie on the other hand, his dad had become more introverted. Mr Beaumont went out to work in the local garage, trained with Charlie in the garden, and that was all. It would be a rare occasion that he should leave the house outside of work hours. Charlie's mom did anything that required a step into the outside world. Millers Fall had one bar called *'The Millers,'* which should of course come as no surprise given the name of the town.

Now, most guys intown clocked off on a Friday evening and spent the rest of the night in the dingy watering hole shooting pool and putting the world to right, but not Mr Beaumont. He had no interested in anyone aside from his family. I always believed that his trust in the community had been diminished, and that he'd witnessed something terrible during his tour, something which changed his outlook on life.

"Anyway, screw that asshole," Chris continued. We settled back down to lunch. "What are we doing this weekend?"

I shrugged and took a bite from my sandwich. Peanut butter and jello, my favourite filling. Mom said it was bad for you, with the sugar from the jam and the fat in the butter. She only made it for me when supplies were low, making this sandwich a sign that grocery shopping wouldn't be too far away.

"Don't know?" I replied, enjoying the sweet and savoury flavours dancing within my mouth. One thing I did know, though, was that somehow during the scuffle my sandwich had been squashed.

Chris relaxed. His shoulders dropped and the anger strewn across his face lifted.

"Guys, this is probably the last time we're going to get to do something, you know?"

Charlie frowned. "What are you talking about?"

"Something good. Like, you know, camping or something? We should go on one last camping trip before the weather gets too bad."

Louis squirmed. "I don't know, it's getting pretty cold out there. I froze my nards off just walking here this morning."

"Ah, come on," Chris whined, "it's our last chance. One more trip up to Rayburn Point. Camp fire, marshmallows, one last night beneath the stars? Winter always drags and we don't ever get to do anything like this for months. Come on. One last camp-out. What do you say?"

"The clearing at Rayburn is covered in trees, idiot. It won't be beneath the stars," Charlie quipped.

"You know what I mean!"

"I can't, not this weekend," I began, still savouring the divine taste of my sandwich. "I got work on Saturday. By the time I finish, get packed up and trek to Rayburn It'll be too dark."

"We can do it for you," Chris started. His reply was instant, like he knew what I was about to say. "We'll take the tent and your stuff in the morning, set it all up and get everything ready. That way you can come straight from work. We can do that, can't we Charlie?"

Charlie looked up from his meal. "Oh, erm, yeah, sure."

Louis looked at me. "Are you going, then?"

"Why not? There's nothing else to do around here."

That evening, I arrived home and told my parents everything I had planned for the weekend. Now, back in '68, and in Millers Fall, it was a far different society to the one that exists today. Everybody knew everybody. Crime intown fell into one of three categories; drunkenness, domestic abuse and shoplifting, and in most cases, the community found out about it before the police did. I know it may seem dangerous as we talk about this today and in our current social state, but back then there was little to no threat of anything happening to a group of kids out camping on the outskirts of town. We played there all the time during the summer months. Well, play is not quite the right word I'd use to describe it.

When we were younger we played in the woods, cowboys and indians, cops and robbers, and built dens pretending they were forts. Our imagination knew no boundaries back then, but as we grew older these games merged into other activities, like fishing, camping and drinking beer that Charlie stole from his dad. Mr Beaumont never went to the bar, remember? That meant his stack of beer inside the kitchen cupboard was larger than most. Charlie, being the sneaky, devious miscreant that he was, waited until the crates had been opened before lifting a few for us to drink. He hadn't been caught stealing beer up to that point, and something tells me he never did.

My parents were fine with me camping, as long as I didn't cut work early. Maintaining obligations was one of the first lessons they taught me, and thus a lesson which served me well throughout my life. So, the next day at school I arranged everything with the guys. I'd take my kit to work, they'd take it to Rayburn Point and pitch up the campsite. I'd then head there once I finished, with the hope that they had indeed pitched everything like they said they would. This meant I didn't need to help out, as pitching a tent happened to be one of my least favourite activities. However, if they were to encounter any problems or a change of plan, one of them would come back to the shop to tell me.

The plan was set.

Chapter 5: Beneath The Stars

I met the guys early on Saturday morning, on Main Street outside Ted's. A typical, autumnal morning found a chilly wind nipping at my fingers as I awaited their arrival. My dark backpack sat at my feet on the sidewalk. I'd managed to fit clothes and boots in there, and strap my rolled sleeping bag to the side.

    The guys arrived on time, and after a brief bout of small talk I handed over my belongings and watched them wander across the park toward the distant woodland. Louis had decided to tag along after all. I knew he would. Even at the age of fourteen, I knew just how strong a bond we all had. Where one went, we all went. That's the kind of friendship I came to miss in my later years.

    Saturday started in typical fashion. Slow to begin with on opening. Ted dressed like your typical barber, white buttoned smock, trousers and shoes. The guy must have been in his early sixties. White hair, white moustache. You know exactly the kind of gentleman I mean. He was *that* guy.

    I started by sweeping the varnished, wooden floor, making sure to reach every corner, every nook and make sure it gleamed once completed. The glaze from the varnish reminded me of the pristine table Mom kept at home. The old brush glided over its surface with ease, taking the clumps of hair in its bristles and leaving them wherever I saw fit.

Usually beside the cash register, as that's where the dust pan and brush were stored, and not far from the trash can hidden in a small hallway leading out back. I then moved to tidying the various products on the shelf. So many. I remember my amazement at how many products had been formulated for men. Shampoo's, soaps, wax, anything and everything need to keep a bonafide gentleman in tip-top condition.

'My Boyfriend's Back' by The Angels bellowed from a small radio into the empty shop. I gave the dark upholstery of the barber's chair a wipe over before doing the same on the leather sofa the customers used whilst awaiting their turn.

Ted emerged from the back with a dollar bill. "Callum, be a sport and run across to Doris' for me. Grab us both a cup of coffee."

"Yes sir," I replied, placing my damp rag on the windowsill before taking the dollar from his hand. Sodas were the usual choice of beverage for most normal fourteen year-olds. Not me. My favourite had been, and always would be, coffee. I loved the strong, rich taste of it. You had to drink it hot, though. Warm or lukewarm did the drink a huge disservice.

The day had started to warm a little since I stood outside gaining frostbite, waiting for my bag to be collected. Sunshine burst from behind the clouds, and the early morning breeze had since subsided. False summer, I always thought. Those rare, autumn days where mother nature throws a curve ball and blesses the world with a cool, summer day before hitting you with gusting winds and rain for months after. The clown at the circus, right? Today Millers Fall had been thrown the bucket of confetti.

Mr and Mrs Norris peeped the horn and waved as they passed by in their Buick Skylark convertible. They though it warm enough to travel roof down. I thought them insane. It could only be for show, I thought. Why ride with the roof down in a cold temperature?

"Morning Callum," Mr Norris shouted over the hum of the engine.

"Good morning," I shouted back. They had a son living in Pittsburgh as far as I knew. An early start out probably meant they were on visiting duty that day.

I stepped from the sidewalk and crossed the road, humming the song that I had been working to just a few moments before. Down the road Doris' Diner had opened. It perched on the corner of Main and King, with a red and white awning stretched along the walls. Generic blinds hung inside the windows, and I noted the opening times on the door as I hopped up the curb and made my approach.

The Angels greeted me again as I stepped inside, suggesting both our radios were tuned to the same station.

"Good morning, Callum," Doris said as I approached the counter. Doris and her husband, Alf, ran the joint where all the hipsters and cool cats liked to hang out. Although, not many of them packed the booths this early in the morning.

Remember, back in '68, diners were the place to be. Most kids hit them on a Friday and Saturday night, meeting for milkshakes after attending a drive in on the outskirts of Butler. But in general, the place could be packed on any given evening.

Doris herself looked as sixties as sixties could get. Black, Tura glasses rested on her nose. False pearls adorned her neck, but it was the large bouffant mass of dark hair that secured the look. I mean, it was huge. I marvelled at how circular the mass had been styled. Almost perfect. I'd been drawing shapes for years, and even I couldn't draw a circle as perfect as the mound that adorned her head. Yes, sir. If they ever decide to use pictures in the dictionary, you'll find the word 'sixties' with her portrait beneath.

"I take it you want the usual?"

"Yes please."

"Coming right up." She turned and found a couple of polystyrene cups.

Alf emerged from the kitchen and joined Doris behind the counter. "Hello, young sir. How are you?" he asked, wiping his hands on an already oil-soiled apron.

"I'm good, thank you. Getting ready for another day."

"Anyone in yet?" he asked as Doris filled the cups on the counter.

"Not yet. Just grabbing a drink before the madness starts."

She added milk to them both. "Fifty cents please."

I handed across the dollar.

Alf leant down on to the white counter. "Say, did I hear right that your dad is overseeing the development in Ellwood?"

I nodded. "Yes…well, kinda. They've had some trouble with the structures over there, so he's gone into check the blueprints and make sure everything's alright."

Doris handed me the change. "Clever fella you're old man," she said whilst adopting the exact same pose as her husband. "I think we're gonna need to get him into sort some of our building work out. How about mom? Is she okay?"

Mom had been involved in an automobile accident a year or so before. She'd been travelling back into Millers Fall when some silver haired old fart in a Pontiac pulled out from a side road and ploughed straight into her. She'd suffered a broken leg and undergone corrective surgery. Dad had taken time out to look after her, and she'd taken an age to recover. She eventually did, except for a minor limp she'd accrued for her troubles. And my Dad, knowing that his wife could now get around without any trouble, eased himself back to work. The job in Ellwood had been the perfect start.

"She's getting there," I said, playing down the limp.

"Well, send her our best, and tell her were having a get together next Saturday evening. She's more than welcome to come along."

I pocketed the change and took hold of the drinks. "Yes, ma'am, I will."

"Alright. Have a good day, now," Alf said as I turned to leave.

"You too."

Back outside, I stepped on to the sidewalk, avoiding the cracks and uneven surfaces I'd memorized. Like I said, coffee is my divine nectar. If I dropped it I'd be pissed.

A car passed by, and with an empty road behind it I took the opportunity to make my way across. It was at this moment that I noticed two bodies heading toward me. They passed the barbers and came to stop in front of the alley that led behind it, blocking my path.

"Holy shit! Would you look at this moron right here." My heart sank. Of all the people in all the world that could have crossed my path at that exact moment, I'd been unfortunate enough to draw Troy Peller and his right-hand man Billy Brewster. God knows what these two assholes were doing around town at a little after nine in the morning on a Saturday, but it couldn't have been anything good. My hands carried hot drinks. Peller smirked, and with one swift movement grabbed my smock at the neck. I tussled, attempting to break free, but with two coffee's in either hand I fought at a disadvantage. He threw me into the small alley beside the barbers. I crashed into an unforgiving wall, dropped the cups and spilled their contents across my white uniform.

"He was giving you some real shit the other day," Brewster said, recalling the incident at recess. Billy Brewster was no slouch himself, second only to Troy in stature. The wrestling buddies often rough handled kids at school, and after the aggravated verbal assault and pushing matches we'd engaged in just a couple of days before, I didn't expect them to offer a hearty handshake and 'how do you do?' the next time our paths crossed. Unlucky for me, that just so happened to be at a time I walked alone, holding two damn cups of coffee.

"Yes he did, and now he ain't got his friends around to help him," Peller observed.

Brewster chuckled. "Poor Callum got no friends."

In that moment Troy's arms morphed into tree trunks. He grabbed my neck and thrust me against the wall once again.

"Get off me!" I growled. Of course, at this moment I was scared shitless, but there was no way I would let him know it. Fight or flight. Stand tall.

Troy leaned in closer. So close, in fact, that I noticed a cluster of small freckles on his nose for the first time.

"I'm going to give you a message. I want you to deliver it to your boyfriend, Chris."

Air expelled from my body. I crashed into a garbage can and slumped to the ground. He'd hit me so hard in the stomach I thought it had burst. I coughed and squirmed on the cold tarmac. Each breath that expelled brought with it a blunt, cramp-like pain where I had been struck. These two idiots were not the only danger in the alleyway, though. Broken glass glistened around me, stating it's purpose of intent should my flesh fall on top of it. A rogue sheet of newspaper danced past on the wind, looking to escape the scene without being involved.

Troy cackled. "Get up, you little fuck! I've got a message for Louis and Charlie, too!"

"Kick his ass!" Brewster screeched.

Troy reached down, pulling me to my feet once more. Another swift punch to my body forced more air from lungs, and this time I cried out. The second shot hurt more than anything I'd ever experienced to that point in my life. His fist had caused pain so bad I was sure something had ruptured.

"What the hell is going on here?"

I crashed to my knees as Troy released his grip. Ted stood with us in the alley. My god-damned saviour.

"It's his fault! He started it!" Troy screamed, pointing an accusing finger in my direction. "He tried to take our coffee's-"

"Don't give me that crap, young man! I know damn well you're lying." Ted wandered over and helped me to my feet.

"No I'm not! He barged into us on purpose!" Troy exclaimed, protesting his innocence.

Ted frowned. "Troy Peller, I gave Callum the money to go across the road and buy us both a drink, so stop your bullshit and apologise!"

"What?"

"Apologise. Right now."

Troy snarled. "No way. I'm not saying anything to that little douche."

"Young man, you'll apologise this instant."

"Or what?" Troy smirked. "What're you gonna do about it, huh?" Ted placed a protective arm around me as Peller continued the back chat. "That's what I thought, old man. Nothing. You're gonna do absolutely nothing."

Ted turned back. "What do you think is going to happen next time you and your dad come in for a haircut, and I tell him you've been banned?"

Troy's smirk disappeared. There was only one person in the world that he feared, and that was his father.

I entered the shop and sat on the couch I'd been wiping not ten minutes before.

"Are you alright?" Ted asked, helping me down. I felt like I'd been smashed by a 16-wheeler somewhere between San Francisco and San Diego, and landed here in Pennsylvania.

"Yeah, yes I'm okay."

Some memories and feelings you experience vanish as you get older, but what I felt after that beating has remained with me my whole life. To this day I can still recall the pain surging through my body at that moment. Damn Peller and his opportunistic punches.

"Just take it easy for a moment. I'll get your parents…"

"No, no. It's okay. Honestly." I knew the pain would only last a while. At least, I hoped it would. "I'll be alright. Just give me a minute."

Outside, Troy and Brewster peered through the window. They both flipped us off before spitting on the glass. "Goddamn, I hate that kid," Ted said to me as he watched them run away.

I laughed, exacerbating the pain. "Everyone does."

As the morning wore on, my pain subsided, and by lunch time, except for the odd, blunt strain here and there, I'd almost forgotten I'd been attacked. I swept the cuttings, tidied up in Ted's wake and just helped out with whatever he needed. By 1pm we'd started to slow down, and by 2pm the shop had become empty. Ted and I peered out of the window, with nothing more to do except watch the world go by. Just down from us, before Doris' Diner, the convenience store stood as we did, open for custom, but neglected by those who walked by. An oversized star-spangled banner hung above its entrance and waved in the invisible breeze, it's end frayed after years of weathering. Across the road the park bustled. That warm sunshine I'd experienced on my trip up to Doris' had decided to stick around, and the townsfolk were making the most of it.

"Well, would you look at that?" Ted said, drawing my attention away from the people enjoying the weather.

"What?"

He pointed down the road. "Just there. You see him?"

I followed Ted's finger and peered along the street. A man had stopped on the kerb waiting to cross the road. He bore a scruffy beard down to his waist. Army camouflage clothing covered his body, and beneath his cap sprouted curled, white hair.

"Is that...Is that Lonesome Jones?"

Ted nodded. "Sure is."

Lonesome Jones had become the Millers Fall version of Sasquatch, and something of a local legend, so to speak. No one knew anything about him, except that he lived within the dense woodlands that surrounded the town. It was rare to see him. In my fourteen-year existence this was only the second time I had laid eyes on him.

"He must need something," Ted began, "or he wouldn't be down here. You know, every time he walks past he looks in, and I offer him a free haircut. He just waves and walks away."

"Have you seen him much?"

"Not really. Once a year, twice if I'm lucky."

The elusive old hermit began across the road, his beard plastered against his body. He found himself the subject of many stories circulating the town. Some said he had murdered his entire family back in the forties but no bodies had ever found. Some said he was an eccentric millionaire living in a hidden shack somewhere. I even heard stories that he had become the guardian of some kind of treasure hidden deep within the woods. I watched as the unkempt wizard made his way toward our shop, knowing full well he'd just walk past. There had been accounts of people attempting to follow him over the years, but somehow he'd lose them once he entered the woodland. Note to self. Never play hide and seek with Lonesome Jones. Only one person is better than him... Bigfoot.

After a moment the old man appeared outside the shop, peering in, just as Ted had explained. His gaze fell upon mine, and piercing, green eyes glared at me through the window. His expression was one of judgement, and made me uncomfortable. After a few seconds his gaze shifted to Ted.

"Come on," Ted began, pointing to the chair. "Come in and let me sort that hair out for you?"

Lonesome lifted his hand, waved, and continued his journey. I watched him as long as I could before he vanished from sight.

"Creepy guy," I said aloud, remembering the stare he'd given me.

"Not creepy. A little mad, maybe, but not creepy."

I argued Ted's opinion. That glare, those eyes, the way he looked at me. It was creepy, if not a little frightening.

Just before 4pm, I noticed movement outside the window. Chris loitered on the empty side walk. Ted had noted this already and wandered over to the till. The register pinged open and the old man handed me my wage for the day.

"Go on, Callum. There's not going to be much footfall this close to closing time."

I took the money and shoved it into my trouser pocket. "Are you sure? There's still time?"

Ted smiled and waved me away. "If there is, it's nothing I can't handle by myself. Go on, have a good evening, now."

I thanked Ted, removed the apron and threw my jacket on top of my brown and white t-shirt.

"Hey, is everything okay?" I asked Chris, stepping into the early evening chill.

"Fine. I just thought I'd come down and meet you."

Whatever Charlie brought to our group, the eccentricity, the impulsive decisions, the unpredictability and so on, Chris countered with the opposite. In general, he expressed a calm persona, except of course when confronted by Peller. Troy brought out the worst in my friend. He unleashed an anger unlike anything I'd ever seen. Chris had been Troy's number one target since we started school, and things were brewing. In these situations you get the feeling that hostilities will escalate the longer they proceed, and we all knew Chris was about ready to take the next step.

It was a huge contrast to the kid we knew. Yes, he had trouble at home, but it wasn't his fault, and like a trooper he continued on no matter what life threw at him. He had no affinity toward his mother since her slump into depression, but he took care of her. He made at least one meal a day for the both of them, even if it was something as simple as a ham sandwich. He washed the clothes and made sure she took her pills, often saying it was pointless her taking them. It was his attendance at school that I respected him the most for. Any other kid in his situation would flat out refuse to attend, knowing there would be no consequences at home.

If I had no consequences, I'd sure as hell spend my days doing whatever I liked, reading books, drawing, watching TV. The world would be my oyster. But he never took advantage of the situation. He kept attending. Not even sickness would keep him away. One time he got struck down with the flu. He stumbled into school looking like he'd gone twelve rounds with Joe Frazier. His eyes sunk back in their sockets, his pale skin glistened with sweat, and yet there he was. Sat in math, shivering away to himself beneath a faded, grey sweater. I think that school was his escape. It gave him a way of feeling like a normal fourteen year-old kid for a few hours, even if he did have to put up with all that crap from Troy Peller.

We crossed the road and headed into the park, walking along the path that cut from one side to the other. I explained what had happened earlier that day with Troy and his sidekick.

"He's such an idiot. One day he's gonna get what's coming to him. It's a shame we all hadn't been there with you. Four against two and I think he'd have thought differently," Chris surmised. I agreed with him. Troy had never attempted to fight any of us when we were together, not seriously anyway, which made him a snake. Laying in the grass, striking his prey when they least expected it.

"Four against three," I quipped. "Louis would be hiding in the trash cans."

"Ain't that the truth," Chris chuckled. Louis. God, I loved that kid, but he was more of a fourteen year-old girl than most of *the* fourteen year-old girls we knew. Which, in our case, wasn't that many.

Chris explained to me everything the guys had done during the day as we reached the outskirts of town and headed into the woodland. The temperature had dropped since earlier that afternoon, and my breath appeared ahead of me as I spoke. Somewhere over to the west Lake Medina rested. Back in the summer it was a great place to go fool around for the day, swimming, relaxing, all that kind of stuff, but at the back end of autumn with a wind that howled across it surface and freezing waters, it was not ours, nor anyone else's first choice of a fun-filled destination. Well, with the exception of the dog walkers that is. But we all know a dog walker. Tough as nails. Nothing deters them. Hell, I bet a dog walker could traverse through Antarctica with nothing more than a good winter coat and a ball to keep their mutt entertained.

I hadn't been out this far from Millers Fall in a while, since mid-summer at least. The often-walked trail we found ourself wandering had vanished beneath a litter of brown, orange and red leaves. Spiked, empty branches reached out from all directions as we wandered between the mass of naked trunks. Wind eased past in a gentle but biting breeze. To me, it felt colder the further we travelled from civilization. If the forecast for tonight was correct, and the sky was indeed clear, our camping trip would become colder. *Much* colder.

We continued on the trail as the light dwindled and faded. At this point I appreciated

Chris being beside me. I'd have made it up to Rayburn Point on my own, but something about the woodland during nightfall made me a tad uneasy. Lots of darkness up there, lots of shadows. Who knew what lurked between the trees?

Soon enough the looming pines appeared, all of which filled my nose with their wonderful, pungent aroma. But, with each step, the woodland became denser, and denser meant darker. Just up to the right I noticed Old Man's Claw, a rock formation with a jagged edge that pointed to the left. Old Man's Claw, so named by someone from decades past, for whatever reason. It didn't bare any resemblance to a claw, or an old man for that matter, but it did play an important role in the journey.

To the left of the trail, the pines clustered together. Opposite the jagged rock a small trail could be found, if you pushed through the pines far enough. Most hikers wandered past without noticing anything different, but to those of us who knew, it was a pathway to a secluded opening beside a rushing river. Our clearing. Rayburn Point. Staying on this track for a quarter mile would lead to a split, and you could take a different trail leading to a towering wall of limestone. An opening in the rock housed another walkway that locals called Moonshine Alley, another Millers Fall legend rarely seen. Moonshine Alley drew its name from the white glow its walls omitted when exposed to the unbroken beam of a full moon. We'd never seen it, but then again we never left our campsite after dark to witness it, either.

I followed Chris through the dense greenery and fading light until voices drifted to us from a clearing ahead. Charlie and Louis laughed about something. The campfire flickered amber and white, creating a dancing shadow across the canvas of the pitched tent.

I'd arrived.

Our final night in the great outdoors could now commence.

Chapter 6: Chris Lester

Chris Lester had been my friend as long as I could remember. Yes, we had our fallouts and arguments, but what friendship didn't? Like I said, he projected himself in the opposite manner to Charlie. They both shared a healthy dose of self-confidence, but unlike Charlie, Chris wouldn't make an ass of himself for any reason.

During any type of confrontation that happened between the four of us, verbal or physical, and also with kids at school he didn't know, Chris always stepped into make sure no fists were thrown. Although his dislike for Troy Peller surged throughout his veins, he never wanted it to escalate to violence. As time wore on, though, we all saw that a confrontation with Troy and his pal Billy loomed on the horizon.

I lost count of how many fights Chris had stopped at school, and credit to him for doing it. He could brawl with the best of them, for sure, but he hated it. He'd rather let someone talk shit to him and walk away than engage in combat. One Sunday last year we'd been hanging out in the park when a couple of older kids from out of town had started picking on Louis. Louis had drawn the short straw and been charged with running to the store to grab us all a soda. We all chipped in, handing him the shrapnel of coins we could muster, and like a hobbit with a magic ring Louis began his journey to McGruder's Conveniences.

The older kids had been playing football and, Louis being Louis, unaware of his surroundings, had wandered through their field of play. The ball was thrown to a kid playing wide receiver, but it never reached him. Louis saw the ball hurtling toward him. His instinct kicked in and within a second he'd made an interception that Lem Barney of the Detroit Lions would have been proud of. Of course, the older kids didn't regard this in quite the same manner. He'd stopped a sure-fire touchdown, and they were pissed.

One of the larger kids berated Louis for becoming involved. Louis apologised, but it hadn't been enough for the kid screaming. He took Louis by the collar, shouted in his face and threw him to the grass. We'd been watching the whole incident unfold, and within a second Chris had leapt to his feet and sprinted to Louis' aid. Chris screamed something offensive and before we knew let his fists loose. The guy fell unconscious on the floor, struck by a killer hook to the chin. This, of course, wiped the smiles from the rest of his friends' faces, and they watched on as Chris helped Louis stand up. After that, we never saw those out-of-towners again.

This period of time for Chris found him thinking a little differently, though. His dad had been declared missing in action, and that brought with it a host of emotions, fear being the strongest. Chris idolised his father, and that was something I never really understood. Don't get me wrong, it wasn't like Mr Lester was a bad father, he just never expressed any interest in Chris or what he was doing.

Sometimes, I felt that Chris had a need to prove himself, like he had to earn his dad's respect, but no matter what he did the outcome remained the same. Families, eh? All so different, and in some cases all so weird. It's like playing poker. You get dealt a hand, and that's the hand you play with for the rest of your life. Damn, it'd be so much easier if you could pick the cards you wanted instead of the ones dealt to you. Same with your family members.

Hidden beneath his clothes Chris wore a ring on a twine necklace. He didn't know what type of ring it was, just a simple, silver band with no markings. What he did know, though, was that ring meant something to his father. On the day his dad left for service, he gave it to him to look after. That ring meant the world to Chris and he'd protect it with his life if he had to.

Chapter 7: Camping

The tent itself was nothing more than a dark green prism large enough to house us all and our bags. I said my hello's and asked Louis if he'd dressed for winter. He informed me that thermals were already in play beneath the trousers. Charlie directed me to my bag, which had been placed inside the tent and out of harm's way. I stepped inside, found my belongings and dropped my pants. Mom would lose her mind if I went home with my best trousers plastered in mud and crap, so I packed my outdoor attire of old jeans and a red shirt. Outside, the river rushed past about twenty feet away. It hissed and splashed past over a bed of limestone and rocks on its way down to join Lake Medina.

    A short while later, I emerged from the tent to a roaring fire which been established between two large logs, giving us all somewhere to sit and keep warm. Chris and Louis perched upon one, and Charlie the other. I made my way across and sat down beside him. He scooted across. The daylight decayed at a rapid rate, but the fire threw out light as well as warmth.

    "Chris told us about Troy," Charlie said, settling himself back down. The memory of those swift punches to my stomach flooded back.

    "Ah, don't worry. I'm over it," I replied.

    Louis threw a small stick into the flames. "It's not fair, though. What's going to stop him doing that shit again if he wants to?"

"Look, don't worry about him," Chris began. "Everyone at school hates him. He only has Brewster as a friend, and that kid is too dumb to know any better. If Troy tries to start something again next week, we'll all just pile him. He can't take four of us down, even if Brewster steps in."

"Guys," I started, knowing full well that this could be our topic of discussion for the remainder of the night, "we came up here because this is our last weekend to camp out. I don't want to ruin it by talking about that asshole. Let's just have a good time, alright?"

Charlie slapped his knees and saluted. "Message received, Captain. Louis, let's start the party." Louis leant down to the bag at his side and produced a large jar of hotdogs, proudly displaying them like the father of a newborn baby.

"Your dad is going to have your ass," Chris chuckled. It was a well-known fact that Louis' father enjoyed this particular delicacy, more so than the average human being. In fact, a missing jar of hotdogs from the Johnson household would be enough to launch a full-scale search and rescue, if, of course, Mr Johnson had his way.

In an even prouder father moment, Charlie produced us each a can of Iron City. "Dad's having beers tonight. Mom will probably think he drank them all in one go, and he won't remember a thing come tomorrow morning."

Iron City wasn't my drink of choice, I have to admit. But, one that's under age and with your best friends on a camping trip? Hell, I'd drink to that, even if it did taste like camel piss.

He passed the aluminium cans around whilst Chris passed us each a branch he'd crafted to a skewer. Louis then opened the jar in which our banquet awaited, took a sausage and passed the jar to me. I took one, impaled it and thrust my meal into the fire before passing the jar to Charlie. Chris passed around an old army canteen that we chugged water from. We'd save the beers for later.

We chatted about school, about girls, TV, comics, all the general things a fourteen year-old tends to talk about when surrounded by their best friends. I quizzed Charlie on his feelings for our school pin-up Erica Ricketts. He laughed, telling me he'd never have a chance at dating her the conventional way. His plan from the start had been to wind her up so bad that she'd agree to a date just to get him off her back.

I didn't think Charlie needed to stoop to this kind of method, though. He was a very good-looking guy. Even myself as a heterosexual male could look at him and know that. He had those soft, almost feminine features I could see adorning the cover of *Teen Set* magazine. His biggest downfall came by association. He hung with us, a group of average guys regarded as nothing more than classmates. Even that was a push. If Charlie had been on the football, basketball or wrestling team there'd be no shortage of girls hanging from his arm, of that I was certain.

We lost track of time setting the world to right and drinking our beer. This time it tasted sweeter, and I drank my way through it without having to pour any on the ground. Does stolen beer taste better? It was a plausible theory I found myself pondering over. Maybe that was the alcohol, though? A fourteen year-old, unable to hold his drink could think a lot of weird shit as he took the first steps toward being drunk.

Before we knew it night had engulfed the woodland. The river rushed somewhere nearby, hidden behind a thick veil of natural darkness. After a bout of roasted marshmallows, again lifted from the Johnson residence, we sat in silence, listening to the water hiss and splash. The clouds hadn't lifted like the forecast had informed me, so it wouldn't be as cold as I was expecting. Still cold, though, just not frostbite-in-your-dick-if-you-go-to-piss cold. The wind danced through the surrounding trees, swaying branches and rustling their leaves.

"How long do you think the war will last?" Chris asked, to no one in particular. It was an awkward question. None of us liked talking about the war, especially with his dad's situation still unresolved.

"I think it will end soon," Louis replied, offering nothing more. I guessed it was his attempt at subtle reassurance. Chris prodded a stick into the fire.

"It's a shitty little country that no one cares about. Why the hell did it start in the first place? I mean, there's guys over there, guys like my dad, fighting and dying, and for what? What are they fighting for?"

It was a tough question for a fourteen year-old to ask, and even tougher for a fourteen year-old to answer. Why was his dad sent to the slaughter? I'll tell you; because America feared the spread of communism. At that time I had no idea why the conflict began, let alone what the word 'communism' actually meant.

We knew Chris had become affected by the absence of his father, worrying for his well-being and holding out the hope that he would return home sooner rather than later. With every day that passed, though, Chris' hopes died that little bit more.

Our camp had taken a sombre tone. Louis and Charlie both peered at the ground. I knew it would be up to me to assure him, if he would listen.

"One day, all of this will be over. Everything. And you'll be able to sit with your dad and tell him how you felt. He'll be able to tell you how he felt, too. You've just got to carry on, like he is. Every day that passes is another day closer to his return home. One day at a time, Chris, one day at a time."

I didn't know if my words would help, or if he'd appreciate them, but at that time I felt some reassurance would be better than leaving Chris to stew in his own negativity.

"Yeah, yeah you're right," he said, standing up from the log. "Look at me ruining our last night here in the great outdoors. I'm gonna take a piss then I'll get the cards."

Charlie's face beamed. "Oh yes, that's what I wanted to hear! What are we playing for?"

"Pine cones," Chris replied as he wandered into the trees.

We played cards and told jokes. We laughed. We howled into the sky. Wolf pack forever.

And forever it would be.

Looking back on it, I can say I experienced the greatest night of my life that night. Nothing since has ever been close to how happy I felt being around my friends at that time.

We stayed up until the fire died down, it could have been midnight, it could have been 4am, none of us knew, and we didn't really care. We crawled into our sleeping bags, sealed the tent and went to sleep. As I lay there listening to the river and the trees, I never guessed that this would be the last time our lives would be considered normal.

Chapter 8: Louis Johnson

I awoke to the sound of canvas flapping in a gentle breeze. My groin burned, and if I didn't do something in the next minute or so we'd all be swimming out through the opening. Damn beer. I knew I should have tipped it away when no one was looking. The breeze grazing my arm encompassed me within its deep morning chill. Chris and Charlie remained wrapped inside their sleeping bags. Louis, however, had all but vanished. I sat up, and, doing my best not to disturb both sleeping beauties unconscious beside me, exited the tent into the cold woodland. Louis sat beside a new fire, again dressed up and ready to go explore the arctic circle.

"Hey," he whispered, tending to a camping mug perched upon a rock beside the fire.

"What time is it?" I whispered back, heading toward the nearest bush.

"A little past six thirty," he replied, checking his watch. I released the kracken from his hiding place and began urinating behind the leaves. Steam wafted into the chilly morning air.

"What are you doing up so early?" I asked, joining Louis by the fire once I'd finished.

"I couldn't sleep."

I held my palms to the fire, warming them as the flames began to emerge.

"What are you making?" I asked, nodding toward the cup.

"Nothing, just hot water, that's all. I woke up cold. I really need something to warm me up."

Louis was right. The temperature had fallen lower than it had been when we retired. But, it was still early. The likelihood of it warming a little as the day progressed would be good, that's if the damn clouds rolling in didn't linger around.

Louis winced whilst removing the cup from the stone, placed it on the ground and then wrapped the handle with a white sock.

"That isn't the sock you wore yesterday, is it?" I asked.

Louis smiled. "No way. It's one of my spares." He took a sip and released a long sigh, as though he'd taken his first mouthful of a fresh, cold soda right out of the refrigerator. "It might just be water, but its good stuff." He took another sip before offering the cup to me. Realising just how cold I'd become, I took the cup and downed a mouthful, burning or not. The heat spread through my body in an instant, causing me to shiver.

"Damn, you're right. This is just what I need." I took another drink to warm my old cockles before handing it back.

"I've been thinking, you know?" Louis began, peering up into the trees. "How long do you think we'll be doing this?"

"What?" I asked.

"This."

"You mean camping? Well, today is going to be the last day for the year for me. Its freezing."

"No, not just camping. I mean this; the four of us. Do you think we'll be friends forever?"

His question seemed out of sorts. Louis wasn't known for his philosophical outlook on life. In fact, if he could look past the end of the week he'd be working too hard.

I shrugged. "I guess so. Why wouldn't we be?"

"You know, things. Just…things. Like, our parents could move? We could end up going to college and never seeing each other again? Maybe even get new friends at school? There's so many things that could happen."

Louis had a tendency to focus on the negatives in life. He was the kid that expected the worst to happen in every scenario, whether that be life experiences or medical. If he had a rash, it'd be caused by some kind of virus that caused your dick to fall off. If his mom wasn't back from the grocery store on the dot, she'd had an accident or run away. A headache became a tumour. A detention became a criminal record. That kind of thing.

Sometimes it could be hard being his friend, as the simplest of activities could be blown way out of proportion. You often found yourself having to talk him down from the perch he'd escalated himself up to. In most cases a quick chat worked, but on occasion he would not listen and you just had to hold your hands up and walk away. This irked Charlie, as Louis' whittling could often affect our activities and what we did. Most of our arguments stemmed from clashes between the two.

"Louis, you're like an old man worrying about stuff that may not even happen. You're fourteen, like the rest of us. The only thing I'm worried about is dying a virgin."

"I mean it, Cal. All the good stuff we do might just be memories in a few years' time." He took another drink from the cup and peered into the trees with a thoughtful look upon his face.

I became somewhat confused, and a little concerned as to his new outlook. "Are you okay, Louis?" I asked. My concern must have come across to him. The thoughtful look had now dispersed into that dimpled smile his mother loved.

"Yeah. Yes, I'm fine. I just…I just had a weird dream last night that kind of made me think of things."

I nodded. I didn't know what was floating around inside his head, but I could relate to dreams that made you think.

"You don't need to worry, Louis. Look at it like this; our parents all seem to be settled in Millers Fall. If any of them split up, it's probably going to be our dad's that move out, leaving us with our mom's in the house, so we won't leave town if that happens. Also, none of us are geniuses. I can't see any one of us leaving for college, can you?"

How naïve I was as a kid.

Louis shook his head. "No. Not when you put it like that."

I flashed him my own smile. "So don't worry about it. We've got one last day up here. Have some fun."

"What are we doing today?" a voice asked from the tent. I turned to see Charlie emerge like an elusive sasquatch from a cavernous opening. "Shit it's cold," he said, hugging his arms about his self. Chris followed close behind. Louis held up the cup to Charlie. "It's hot water." Charlie took it and sat beside him.

"What are you two doing up so early?" Chris asked, dropping down beside me.

"Couldn't sleep," Louis replied.

"Needed a piss," I told them.

"You both sound like a pair of old farts," Charlie retorted. He drank from the cup. "So anyway, I heard you say we're going to have a fun filled day out here today. Got any plans?"

"Nope," I replied, shaking my head.

"There's not that much we can do with the weather like this," Chris began. "There's no way I'm going swimming, and we didn't bring anything to go fishing with."

"No. Screw swimming. My balls would be so cold I'd see them when I brush my teeth," Charlie quipped.

"Why don't we pack down and just go explore, or something?" I suggested. "It'll be better than just packing up and going home."

"Like, where?" Charlie asked. "There's not many places around here we don't know about already."

"What about Moonshine Alley?" Louis began. "I've never been to the end of the trail there."

"We could do, but there's nothing more than a dead end," Chris informed him. "It's just a narrow path between two limestone rock faces.'"

"Have any of you been in there, though?" Louis asked us.

"Not all the way," Charlie replied.

"Not far," I added.

Chris shook his head. "No."

"Why don't we just go and see for ourselves, then? I'm not expecting to find any dinosaurs or anything like that down there, but we can go there just to say we've been all the way."

Charlie grinned. "You'd love to go all the way, wouldn't you, Louis?"

Louis blushed worse than a lovestruck school girl latching eyes on her beau. I couldn't help but laugh.

"You know what I mean!" he snapped. His anger came from embarrassment, at least that's what I thought. You had to expect it with Charlie. His mouth struck anytime an opportunity arose, and with an immature sense of humour behind it, not everyone found the funny side.

At that point Moonshine Alley sounded like a great idea. It wouldn't be too taxing, just follow a trail until we couldn't follow it any more.

"I'm cool with doing that," I said, giving the idea my blessing.

"Yeah, me too," Chris replied. "It looks like it might rain anyway. At least we'll have some kind of shelter. And, I want to say I've been there. Moonshine Alley is like our town's local legend.

Everyone talks about it but not many people have been there. I'd feel like a God damned hero."

Packing the tent down didn't take long between us. We ate the breakfast of champions, as in cold hotdogs and marshmallows, put on our outdoor clothing and left everything at Rayburn Point. We'd return back to take it home.

We pushed through the greenery and back on to the trail a short while later. Those dark clouds had decided to stick around after all, and during our trek they opened up, showering us from above. My thick jeans and red waterproof coat did the trick keeping me dry, though. A chill blasted through me every now and again as the autumn winds and rain combined, but for the most part I walked in comfort. Chris wandered just ahead, kitted out similar, except for a green weatherproof jacket. Charlie?

Well, Charlie was Charlie, clad in jeans, a t-shirt and his green combat jacket. How the guy never froze was beyond me. And Louis? Like I said, wrapped up beneath a scarf and hat, with pretty much every item of clothing he owned worn beneath a blue cagoule. As we walked the trail I felt like a member of the merry men, out on an expedition to find Robin Hood.

We wandered along the trail then branched to the left. The tree cover in the canopies above became lighter and the rain heavier. We continued onward, snapping debris with our boots as we marched toward the limestone rock face and the legendary Moonshine Alley. The weather didn't dampen our spirits. We sang songs, told jokes and messed around. Louis, clad in a thousand dollars worth of clothes it seemed, skidded and fell butt first into a mud puddle. I swear I've never laughed as much in my life as I did then. He stood up, plastered in crap that covered his entire ass. He argued that the ground was uneven, that's why he fell. I argued that if he wasn't wearing enough clothes to stop a bullet he wouldn't have lost his balance. We continued, and made memories.

That's what being a kid is all about.

Chapter 9: Moonshine Alley

A huge, gnarled rock face appeared outside the treeline. It towered above us like some great, judgemental leviathan, peering down on insignificant beings. Moonshine Alley split this leviathan in half, allowing anyone and everyone to venture inside and explore. The opening appeared gloomy and ominous. A surge of apprehension passed through my body. Butterfly's fluttered in my stomach as I bore upon the looming, pale rock face towering into the low cloud. Clumps of grass protruded at the trail's entrance. A thin layer of ground fog expelled from inside. Dead, brittle twigs reached out from the foliage. It reminded me of a set from the old Universal Horror movies I adored. In my mind's eye Bela Lugosi drifted out of the gloom clutching a candelabra. He smiled that terrifying, unhinged smile that creeped me the hell out and beckoned us inside with a welcoming palm.

Up until that point, Moonshine Alley had conjured great and mysterious thoughts in my mind, helped by the name it had come to be known by. To me it created the idea of something from olden days, of cowboys roaming the lands, gunfights and small towns built with timber and planks. Why? I don't know. It hardly seems relevant given the name, but cowboys popped into my mind whenever I thought about this place. I guessed that other people may imagine moonshiners running pickups full of illegal, home brewed alcohol back and forth under the cover of darkness, but I liked to believe my mind more creative than the average person.

As I explained before, the name derived from the supposed glow the rock face omitted during the clear nights of a full moon. I myself had never witnessed this, nor had my friends, so to us it had become just a story people spoke about from time to time. It's crazy how your mind can run away with an idea, build upon it and create a mountain where a molehill once stood. Looking at the rock face it was hard to see how it could reflect any light during a bright summer's day, let alone a clear, dark night. But, someone at some time thought it had, and the story had been created and passed along. That's creatives for you. All in a world of their own.

"I've got a confession," came Chris' voice from somewhere beside me. Somehow, I knew what he was about to say. "I've never been here in my life."

"Me either," Charlie replied.

I became a little unnerved. Not at the nature of their confession, but at the fact their apprehension appeared to mirror mine. No one cussed anyone for lying. No one called the other a pussy. At that moment we felt the same way. Nervous.

"I don't know about this," Louis said, echoing my thoughts.

"About what?" Charlie asked.

Louis pointed to the Alley. "This. It just, you know? It doesn't feel right."

"It was your idea," Charlie reminded him, as if pointing the finger of blame would encourage Louis to retract his thoughts.

"We don't have to go if you don't want to," Chris responded. This statement, although intended well, only served to inspire Charlie.

"Come on, guys, we walked all the way here. I just want to see what's in there."

"Nothing much," Chris began. "It just leads to a wall."

"How do you know?" Charlie snapped, turning to him. "You just said you've never been here before?"

"From what other people have said."

"So you'd rather be told what's in there than go and see for yourself?"

"Guy's," I interjected, noting that Charlie's fiery attitude had awoken. "Come on. We're here to have a good time. Let's not argue."

"I'm not arguing, I'm just being honest," Charlie snapped. It was clear that he intended to navigate the trail, apprehensive or not. Did he want to get one up on us all? Probably not, but it was clear that he intended to prove to everyone just how big a dick he had. "I'm going. You guys can wait out here or come with me."

At that point my fate had been sealed. With Chris and Louis more apprehensive about entering, my role as Charlie's support had been secured, whether I wanted it or not. The truth was, I just couldn't let him wander off into Moonshine Alley alone, regardless of my own fear and apprehension.

Charlie began walking. "You coming or not?" he asked over his shoulder. After another burst of adrenaline I began to walk beside him.

"You going?" Chris asked, sounding shocked.

I turned back. "Yeah. It's just a trail. I don't think there's much to worry about." I didn't know who I was trying to convince the most. Chris or myself. It worked though, as he nodded and made his way over.

"Hey wait!" Louis shouted. "What am I going to do?"

Charlie looked over to him and shrugged. "Come with us or wait out here on your own. It's up to you."

Facing a blunt and grim reality, Louis dropped his head and plodded over. We stood a moment longer, peering into the ominous, winding trail ahead.

"This looks like something out of a horror movie," Louis sighed.

Charlie smiled. "Then let's go and find some monsters."

After a few minutes walking the trail, I felt more at ease. The trail itself stood wide enough that we could wander along side by side in pairs. It sheltered us from the rain. I'd forgotten the weather had turned bad on our venture out here. Drops of water fell from protruding stone in the wall, like someone had turned a slow tap on from areas above our eyeline.

That journey became quite surreal. Something felt different. None of us spoke. We walked, and that was all. A strange wind gusted past. Strange as I had no idea how it could exist. The walls reached high into the low clouds. Any breeze should not be able to reach us at ground level, not at that strength anyway, but it did. A few rogue rain drops rippled on my jacket. Nothing happened. We wondered on until another huge wall of uneven limestone appeared in the trail ahead. So the stories were indeed true. Moonshine Alley ended at the base of another vast wall.

"See? Nothing," came Louis voice from behind us. I looked at him. He was terrified, I knew that much from his expression. It appeared as though he'd burst into tears at any moment.

"You okay?" I enquired, noting his distress.

"I'm fine," he snapped, "I just want to get out of here."

I think Chris noted Louis' fear, too. He nodded in agreement. "Okay, let's go. We've seen it for ourselves. There's nothing much else to see. You ready, Charlie?"

"Yeah… yes, let's make a move. God, I'm hungry. I hope my mom is making dinner."

With that sentence Charlie brought some realism back to the situation. No longer we're we exploring a rarely trodden, fantastical world of hidden mysteries, but instead a debris filled pathway between two rocks. As we wandered back conversation began again, and between the moss and shrubbery we walked within, our spirits lightened and we returned to the group of friends goofing around that we had been before.

"Hold up," Chris said, stopping a few feet away. He reached down and began untying his bootlace. "Got a stone ore something in there." He removed his footwear and shook it by the sole. A small, dark stone tumbled out to the ground. "There we are…"

Chris leant over, placed his boot back on and tied the lace. In a split second, Charlie rushed across and pushed Chris from his feet. We began laughing as he fell against the wall. But then, not against the wall… into the wall… floating…

I gasped. "What the hell?"

Chris frowned and stood up. "What's the matter?" he asked, looking perplexed.

"Chris…" Louis began.

"Your floating. How are you doing that?" Charlie said. The three of us peered at him levitating above the trail.

"Floating? What the hell are you talking about?"

"No Chris, it's true. You are," I replied. Never in my life have I seen anything so strange. I mean, David Copperfield later on in the eighties of course, but not one of your best friends along a woodland trail. Not in a million years

"Are you guys crazy. Look." Chris stomped his foot. It thudded against a surface, but still he hovered a foot or so above the ground.

"Oh my God," Louis whittled. That kid was about to explode.

At that moment a spell of nausea rocked me. I could not believe my eyes. Chris hung in the air like Superman. No wires. No camera trickery. There in plain sight for all of us to see. Concern engulfed his face. He must have realized we were not joking.

"No, look guys." Chris stomped and then jumped, landing again in mid-air.

"Wait, stop," I ordered. For some reason, to this day I don't know why, I approached my friend caught in that strange levitation. I took small steps and outstretched my hands, as if I wore a blindfold, expecting to bump into everything around me. I wandered across the trail and stopped just before the rough surface of the stone wall. I couldn't gain my focus. The wall was there, I could see it. But, it wasn't there, because I couldn't rest my hands upon its surface. At that point my heart pounded. I took a leap of faith and pushed at the wet stone. I tumbled forward, gaining my footing but falling against Chris. He steadied me as I returned to my feet.

Louis gasped. "Oh shit, Callum! You too!"

I looked to my feet. They stood upon the decaying trail.

"What the hell did you do?" Charlie asked.

"Nothing. I'm… I'm fine." I looked across to Chris' feet. He wasn't floating, either. We stood inside a recess, nothing more. The ground here sloped upward. Beyond Chris I noticed a new pathway, different to the one we'd just explored, curving its away around some boulders in the opposite direction.

"This is some freaky ghostly-type shit!" Louis exclaimed, his fear almost uncontrollable.

"Wait. Wait a minute," I said, attempting to calm him down. "Look." I stepped back toward my friends, dragging Chris down with me. We took two steps from the slope and arrived back on the original trail. "It's an illusion," I said, sounding more definitive than I intended.

"What are you talking about?" Charlie asked.

I turned around, ascended the verge into the recess and turned back. "Am I floating now?"

"Holy shit!" Chris shouted.

"Relax. It's natural. From the trail it just looks like a wall, but when you get closer, it's actually a recess. There's another trail down here," I said, pointing to my left.

Charlie took a few steps toward me, then, like a drunk man tumbled up the verge as I had.

"Shit," he said, steadying himself. "You're right. It looks like part of the wall from back there."

"Exactly. And because we're on a verge that you can't see properly, it looks like we're floating."

Charlie smiled and jumped back from his position. "It's like magic," he said, jumping back and forth between the trails. Chris joined him in doing so. Louis, however, was not as impressed.

"You guys are making a deal with the devil," he said, frozen to the spot.

Charlie stopped his hi-jinx. "Hey guys," he said, staring down the new walkway, "I wonder what's down there?"

"Uh – uh. No way," Louis stated, shaking his head in defiance. "This is enough shit for me for one day. I just want to go home."

"Hey yeah," Chris began, ignoring Louis' concern. The sense of adventure returned to his voice. "Perhaps there really could be dinosaurs down there?"

"Let's go look," Charlie, said, gushing with curiosity and excitement. "I bet no one has been here before. No one."

At that point my own sense of adventure returned. This was a discovery. A real adventure. Hell, Tarzan could be living down there for all we knew. Any fears I had were swept away with the thought of exploring a new quest to discover what secrets this hidden pathway would reveal.

"Guys-"

Charlie dropped his shoulders. "Louis, the same deal stands as before. You don't want to come with us? Fine. Stay here. We'll be back when we've finished."

At this point I didn't care for Louis' apprehension. But, as usual, ever afraid to fend for himself, Louis stumbled upon the verge and joined us on the new pathway. "Wow," he said upon seeing our new destination. For that moment, at least, he sounded amazed instead of afraid.

Without a moment's hesitation we began our journey into the unknown.

Only later did we wish we'd listened to Louis.

Chapter 10: The Clearing

"What the hell is this?" Charlie asked, peering up into the rolling sky. We followed the hidden trail for a short distance, which had taken us to some kind of circular clearing. I use the word 'clearing' in the loosest context. It looked more like a pit. Again, the limestone walls surrounded us, but overhanging the opening above we could see trees peering over from the edges.

"What do you think is up there?" Louis asked.

"I don't know," Charlie replied, "but I bet no one's seen it."

We wandered into the centre, across a ground abundant in fresh, luscious grass. It was the strangest thing, something I'll never forget. Pine wafted around us, strong and clean. The rain fell from skies, but somehow each drop appeared bright as it passed into this unexplored area. This was the most amazing discovery of my life. Even then, I was certain no one had set foot on the ground we found ourselves standing on. I looked across to Louis. He peered upward, watching the rain flash and illuminate like fireflies as it tumbled down. A smile beamed across his face. Chris and Charlie gazed upward in amazement.

"What the hell is this?" Chris asked, to no one in particular.

"Who cares?" Charlie replied, his gaze transfixed on the light show that flashed and rippled within the raindrops. It reminded me of finding a rogue spider web strand hanging from the washing line, or a branch. When caught in the right light it glowed for a second or so, until the breeze wafted it out of eyeline. That single, solitary flash is there, for just a moment, and then it disappears. Not these lights, though. They danced around in different directions, upwards, sideways, not caring that the rain fell in one direction. Short flashes exploded in silence, like lightning, across the pit opening that towered above us.

"This is the most amazing thing I ever saw," Louis whispered.

I nodded. "Me too."

We became transfixed on the silent light show until Chris' voice brought us back to earth.

"What's that?" he asked, pointing across the way.

The tell-tale rush of the raging river bellowed from a hidden ravine. We wandered over and peered down. The water raged as it hurtled past and into a small, cavernous opening.

"Must flow underground," Charlie stated.

I nodded. "Yeah. I bet it flows past Rayburn Point and down to the lake."

I stood, mesmerised by the water as it raced by.

"You think anyone else knows about this place?" Louis asked.

"I doubt it," Charlie replied. "We stumbled into it by accident. You'd think word would have gotten around by now if someone else had found it."

Louis squatted down and continued to peer over the edge. "We've discovered a new land. We're like explorers, you know?"

I smiled. "I don't think it comes with any type of reward, though."

"I'm not bothered about a reward. I just think it would be fantastic to have my name attached to a discovery."

"Well, we all know that won't happen," Charlie began, turning from the river and surveying the area. "We report it, adults come up here and take all the credit. They get the recognition, we get nothing." I agreed. That's more in line with how the world works. Sad, but true.

Charlie turned back to me. "So what are we going to do? Keep it secret or tell people?"

"Keep it secret," Louis replied in an instant. "Think about it. This could be our place. When we're older, all married and grown up and stuff, we could come here one weekend a year and hang out. No one would know where we are. We could come here to get away from everything."

"Our own secret hideout," Chris added, looking toward me. "We've discovered this. It's our place."

"It's mine."

I jumped.

Lonesome Jones stood just a few feet away, scowling under his mess of a beard. He glared at us with wild eyes.

"This is no place for anyone, let alone four punk kids. You get away from here, now, you hear me?"

"Why?" Charlie enquired.

"This is my home and I ain't having it disturbed by the likes of you."

Charlie sighed. "But…"

"But nothing. Get outta here now, or so help me God I'll kick your ass!"

That was the worst thing Lonesome Jones could have said at that time. When Charlie found himself backed into a corner he always came out fighting. The gauntlet had been laid, and to Charlie that became a challenge.

"No."

Lonesome's wild eyes pierced him. "You'll do as I god damn tell you! Now move!"

He grasped Charlie's arm and attempted to yank him. Charlie scuffled with the old man and pushed him away. "What the hell do you think you're doing? Don't touch me!"

Lonesome walked back toward Charlie, and with a swift motion slapped him across the face. Before we had the chance to respond, Lonesome grabbed a chunk of his hair, pulled him away from the cliff edge and threw him to the ground.

Chris launched at Lonesome, but the old man sent him back with a forceful push. Chris tumbled into Louis, knocking them both down to the sodden grass. I now stood alone.

"I told you! Get out!"

The old hermit lurched toward me with those wild, crazy eyes. Cold hands gripped my throat and pushed deep into my flesh. I gagged as my airway closed and tumbled over, bringing us both to the ground. My head bounced from the damp surface. The old man kept a hold, now using his bodyweight to push deeper into my throat. I flapped, slapping and clawing at him in a feeble attempt to breathe. His eyes gazed into mine, unflinching. An empty, helpless feeling passed through me. This was it...

The pressure eased. Lonesome fell. Something struck him from the front. I drew a huge, wheezy breath and sat up, coughing to clear my throat. God my chest burned, but I drew breath for what felt like the first time in an age. Chris stood there, clutching a rock in his hand.

"Are you okay?" his blunt voice asked, devoid of any emotion.

"Yes," I croaked.

Chris turned his attention back to Lonesome. I looked across as the aggressive old man pushed himself to his knees, his jacket and pants now soiled with mud and grass where he'd fallen. Chris wandered to him. Both Louis and Charlie helped me to stand.

"You okay?" Charlie asked.

I nodded, not wanting to speak and aggravate my burning throat. As I found my footing I watched as Chris stood above Lonesome Jones. The old hermit wiped blood away from a head injury. The thin skin on his forehead had been opened, adorning his face with a mass of crimson streaks. Lonesome peered at his blood-soaked hand before reaching toward Chris, fingers outstretched, each with a trickle of blood running down them.

"Hey Chris, come on. Let's get out of here before he starts again," Louis shouted. Chris didn't flinch. He stood there with an ice-cold glare firmly placed upon the angry, and now defenceless old man.

"Chris, come on, man? We need to get Callum home," Charlie added. For once in his life Charlie spoke sense.

Without hesitation Chris lifted the rock into the air and smashed it down on to Lonesome's forehead. My heart pounded. Lonesome slumped face first to the grass. I wriggled from my friends' grasp and ran to the fallen hermit sprawled out across the sodden ground. Chris' hands trembled.

"What the hell?" I said, watching my friends hand tremor.

Chris turned to me. "He hasn't moved."

"No shit. He'll be out cold. You got him pretty good."

"I don't know why I did it. I don't know why I hit him again."

"You did it to save Callum," Charlie piped from behind. He stood there, cool as a cucumber. "Who knows what this sack of shit would have done if you hadn't stopped him?"

"What if he's dead?" Chris asked.

Charlie shook his head. "He's not dead. You didn't hit him that hard."

"But what if he is?"

"He isn't," Charlie repeated again, his tone somewhat annoyed. "But we have to decide what we're doing with him."

"Leave him here," I began. "What else can we do?"

"We can't do that. He'll come down into town when he wakes up, and he'll know exactly who to look for," Louis whittled.

I nodded. "He came up to the window at work yesterday. Peered right in and had a good glare at me. He knows where I'll be."

"Guys, he still hasn't moved," Chris interjected. He hovered over the fallen body, like a hawk following its prey. "I think he's dead."

Charlie rolled his eyes. "Come on. We just said he wasn't. It was a good hit."

"But what if he is!"

At that moment my heart sank. Chris' eyes filled with tears. He was afraid.

"Okay, okay," I began, holding my palms up. "I'll check. Just hold on." By this time the pain from my scuffle was bearable, and my breathing had settled back into a steady rhythm.

The butterflies returned to my stomach, though, as the seriousness of our situation sank in. My heart pounded in my ears, and I tried to relax by focusing on the tranquil cascade of rushing water that hissed within the ravine. Raindrops rattled the area around us, and no matter how much I focused on their pattering my attention had to be drawn to the task at hand.

I made my way to the fallen man and knelt down beside him. Lonesome collapsed on his front, his head turned to the left. Beneath the dense bristles of the platinum beard I could see his mouth open and agape. Parts of that beard had absorbed the blood running down his face, staining it with dark red streaks and blotches. The strike Chris had connected with had done Lonesome Jones some real damage. The skin around his eye had also been split, and I'm pretty sure I could see bone matter protruding from it.

"He's been hurt pretty bad," I said aloud, but no one responded. I reached first to Lonesome's back and placed my hand against the waterproof camouflage jacket he wore. I expected the old fart to jump up and start another attack, like they do in all the horror movies, but nothing happened. My first thought had been to check his breathing. I knew I could feel him inhale and exhale by placing a hand between his shoulder blades as he drew breath. As I placed my hand down it became clear he wasn't moving. Undeterred, I moved my hand from his coat, and after a moment of hesitation placed my index and middle fingers into the side of his neck. Not feeling a hint of a pulse I pushed down with more force into his skin. The wiry, scrapy bristles of his beard tickled the back of my hand, making me more uncomfortable. I prodded at a different point of his neck. That's when I panicked.

"What is it, Callum?" Louis asked.

I removed my hand and looked up to them. "He *is* dead," I whimpered.

Chris stumbled back, placing his hands atop his head.

"No, no," he gasped. "No way!"

At that point I witnessed something I'd never seen before. The usual calm, collected and fearless Chris Lester began to cry. His eyes wrinkled and mouth curled as a trickle of tears fell down his cheeks.

"No way, man! No way!" he sobbed.

"We're murderers! Murderers!" Louis screamed.

"Alright, alright! Stop!" Charlie snapped. He stood between them, his arms outstretched, palms outward. Louis managed to gain some composure. Chris not so much.

"I am going to be in so much shit!" Chris warbled.

"We all are!" Louis snapped.

"Damn it! The pair of you! Shut the fuck up!" Charlie blasted. Chris panted, and after a few breaths managed to compose himself.

"What are we going to do?" I asked, staring down at the lifeless body sprawled out upon the grass.

Charlie turned away, placing a hand on his hip and the other on his forehead. The rain fell heavy and fast, as if this were a sign of things to come. "I've got an idea."

"We've got to go to the police. We have to report this," Chris whispered, his eyes still glazed.

Charlie looked to him. "Like hell we do, Chris. Like hell we do."

"Of course we have to," I began, "we've committed a crime. We've committed murder!"

"That's right!" Charlie snapped again, turning to face me. "And you know what will happen? We'll all get arrested and spend the rest of our lives in prison. We may even get the chair or the injection. You want that? Do you? Because I don't. Not when we were just defending ourselves from that piece of shit. If we go to the police we're done for. All of us. We're all accomplices. We're all involved. We can kiss our asses goodbye."

We stood in silence. The cold rain matted my hair.

"What about your idea," Chris said to Charlie. "You said you had one?"

"Yeah, I do. But, we'll all need to remain quiet. Say nothing to no one. Understand?"

"I don't know, guys," Louis whittled once more. "This is really bad. Someone needs to know-"

"God damn it, Louis!" Charlie screamed. "If this gets out we're all in for it. Weren't you listening? If you go running home and tell your parents, you're not just involving yourself, you're getting us into trouble as well! Fuck sake! You need to keep your mouth shut, understand? Because if you don't, I swear to God I'll shut it for you!"

"Alright guys, this isn't the time to be fighting," I said, trying to cool Charlie's hot head. "What's the plan?"

Charlie drew a few breaths and his ice cool calmness returned. "Right, think about this. Lonesome Jones is known all over town. Everyone knows he lives up here, but no one knows where. Everyone also knows that he doesn't come into town very often, only when he needs something. People probably talk about him more than they actually see him."

"That's right," I said, confirming for myself that Charlie was correct. "Ted told me that they see him once every ten months or so, if they're lucky. He said that Lonesome only went to town if he needed medicine or something."

Charlie pointed in my direction. "That's right. Now, that piece of shit was intown yesterday, looking through your window, right? So everyone has seen him. That gives us ten months at least. Everyone knows he's lived up here like, forever. He has no family and no friends. He's an old fart. If he never turns up again no one is going to think anything of it. They'll just assume he's either moved on or died up here. No one will think that we're involved. No one."

"But what if someone finds him?" Chris asked.

"Chris, no one will. How long have people been coming up to Moonshine Alley? How many people have found the track that leads here? No one has ever spoken about this place before. This is why no one could ever find Lonesome when they followed him. He's probably got a shack or a tent somewhere in here that we haven't found. That's why he came out. He must have seen or heard us coming into this place."

"But someone could still find it," Chris argued.

Charlie wandered away for a moment. He looked over the ravine at the river. "I've got it. We throw him down there into the water."

"What good is that going to do?" Louis argued.

"For God sake, Louis! The river runs underground. The chance that the body will emerge from the cave is going to be slim, and even if it does he has a head injury. If anyone was to find him it would look like he had a fall."

"And that would make it look like he had an accident," I added, understanding my friends line of thinking.

Charlie nodded. "Right. It's the only chance we have."

Louis sighed. "I don't know. Why can't we leave him here? No one ever found him until we did."

"Will you stop being an idiot and listen!" Charlie screamed. "There is always a chance he could be found here. And if he is, whoever finds him will know he's been killed by the head injury. At least if we throw him in the river we can make it look like it was an accident."

"And that's even if his body makes it out of the cave," I pointed out.

Charlie's plan made perfect sense, and even more importantly it could absolve us of anything to do with the murder we'd assisted in.

I followed Charlie to Lonesome, grabbed hold of his feet while Charlie took hold of his wrists, and attempted to lift him from the ground.

"God damn he weighs more than a car," Charlie quipped.

I turned to the others. "Guys, come on." They both appeared hesitant, but after a moment Chris moved over and took hold of a leg. As if following the masses, Louis then helped by taking hold of a sleeve, too, being careful to avoid the blood on Lonesome's hands.

"This is gross!" he grimaced.

"Not as gross as what they'll do to you in prison," Charlie said to him.

We dragged the body across the grass to the ravine. Unable to throw him over, we placed him down and rolled the body over the edge. Lonesome smashed into the rocks below, and for a second I thought he'd be stuck in place. After a moment the water took hold and swept his limp body away, into the cave and out of sight.

We stood like statues in the rain, all terrified of what had just happened. No one said a thing. Everything at that moment became surreal, like viewing your life through a TV screen. Not real, but at the same time very real. The world stopped for me there and then, and I hung in a time-zone submerged in dread and disbelief. That few seconds of madness would now taint us for the rest of our lives. As unbelievable as it felt, I knew it was no nightmare, and that I wasn't going to awaken back in the tent with an insatiable urge to pee like I had earlier that morning. This was real life. We were really standing in a secluded clearing, and we had really committed a terrible crime.

I watched as the river flowed past, listening to it roar as it surged into the darkened mouth of the open cave. Something caught my eye in the grass at my feet. I reached down, and of all things I grabbed a penny. The shiny, bronze coin looked so out of place in the clearing that I was surprised none of the others had noticed it. I expected it to be plastered in mud, but instead Mr Lincoln shone back with immaculate pride, gleaming like he had just left the mint and entered into circulation. It must have belonged to Lonesome, as I had left my wages in my work trousers back at camp. I considered throwing it into the river, but something made me stop. What, I don't know, but at that moment I didn't have the heart to dispose of it. A coin. A shitty, little, pointless coin. I took it with me as we left, ensuring no trace of our presence had been left behind.

The rain thrashed down as we headed back to Rayburn Point. Those dark clouds I'd noticed earlier that morning had decided to stay with us, showering heavy, cold rain throughout the woodland. Our parents knew we'd be on our way back, that was always the rule with bad weather. Come straight home. Don't pass Go. Do not collect two hundred bucks.

We collected our belongings from Rayburn Point, headed back out to the trail and picked up the route back to town, traversing the entire journey in silence. This journey felt more like the stories I'd heard from Europe during World War II. Platoons of soldiers walking from one point to the next, always at threat from an enemy that may be watching. Chris bore an expression of stress and anxiety, looking much older than he had first thing that morning.

Louis bore similar pain upon his brow, but not to the extent that Chris displayed. I just hoped he kept that worry-a-minute mouth of his shut. If anyone would squeal, It'd be him. Charlie? Well, he just looked like Charlie. If he'd been upset by what we'd done he hid it well. Me? It felt like I carried a brick in my stomach. I couldn't process what had happened or comprehend what I was going to do. The only thing I knew for certain was that I had changed. From that point onward I became a new person, and not necessarily for the better.

We entered town and made our way to the park, where we'd then proceed to head our separate ways.

"Okay, this is it," Charlie said, bringing us to a stop. He stood strong, like a leader, taking control of a situation we had no experience in handling. The clouds rolled the deepest colour of grey I had ever witnessed, adding to my already increased sense of anxiety. Rain lashed down, bouncing from the grass and forming waterlogged puddles in patches on its surface. "Drop your bags."

We did as Charlie asked, and before I knew anything we huddled with our heads together. I placed an arm over Chris and one over Louis.

"This is it," Charlie began, like a team captain giving a prep talk before a match. "From now on in we have a secret to keep. We need to make right here, right now, a promise to each other that we will never mention this to anyone else. Never. From now on we're all bound to one another. Like a brotherhood. We're the Wolf Pack. We're here for each other until the day we die. Understand? Until the day we die."

"Yes."

"Yes."

"Yes," I repeated.

Chris and Louis would leave one way, Charlie and I another. I slapped Chris with five, and then Louis, before beginning the long walk home. Louis owned the tent we camped in, and although it consisted of thin pipes and a light canvas, it would be too heavy for him to carry alone. Chris helped to transport it back, leaving Charlie and I to head on our own way.

Again, we remained speechless until he bid goodbye, heading his own way home. I wandered on, in my own little dream, oblivious to the world around me. It didn't matter where I looked, the body of Lonesome Jones invaded my mind. I felt angry at him. Why did he have to start fighting? If he'd have kept his fists to his self we'd have left in peace and never returned. Damn that old bastard. It was all his fault. Damn Charlie, too. If he hadn't been so stubborn and pig-headed, we could have just left, leaving the old bastard alone.

A blip and a red light through the rainfall drew me back to reality. I stopped as a police car pulled up, hissing as it slowed through the surface water. The window rolled down revealing Deputy Willis, a slim lady with flowing blonde hair.

"Hey Callum, what're you doing out in this?" she asked. Anxiety surged throughout my being.

"Walking home," I replied, sounding so calm I impressed myself.

"That's a big bag you're carrying, where have you been?"

"Just up to Rayburn Point. We camped there last night. We were going to stay for the day but the rain put a stop to that."

"Did you go with Charlie Beaumont? I saw him not long ago, carrying a bag like yours."

"Yes I did. And Chris, and Louis."

She smiled. "Would have been fun if it wasn't for the rain. That's the problem with this time of year. The weather never plays ball."

"No, it doesn't," I replied. That damn circus clown with the bucket of water just wasn't giving me a break, on today of all days.

"Well, hop in and I'll take you home. I was heading up to yours anyway."

"Why?"

"I need to speak with your dad. You know, family stuff."

"Oh. Okay." I opened the rear passenger door and threw my bag into the car. "Sorry, but I'm going to get the seats all wet."

Willis chuckled as I closed the door. "Don't worry, it's not the worst thing those seats have been covered in."

And there it was. Less than two hours after committing the most terrible of all crimes I was hitching a ride home in a police car with the deputy sheriff of the town. I guess now would be a good time to fill you in on something. If committing a murder wasn't bad enough, I now had to contend with Deputy Willis, and she would never go away. You want to know why?

Because Deputy Willis was my aunt.

Chapter 11: My Current Situation

The best thing about dying, if there is such a thing, is that should you time it right, you receive treatment usually reserved for royalty. Take me for instance, I'm sat in a hospital in my own private room. I have a TV and an en suite, meaning I don't need to share the bathroom with any other fucker on this ward. It's a pain in the ass having to drag a UV full of medication everywhere you go. I'm wired up like a New York City Christmas tree, being pumped full of every drug known to man just to give me a few more hours on this mortal coil. That's the position I find myself.

My time is coming, and sooner rather than later. People come and go. Doctors with their fancy tablets and devices, whispering to each other whilst taking notes, then talking to me like I'm a three year-old kid that doesn't grasp the English language. The ward outside is busy with the medical teams walking here and there, making God-like decisions with the click of a pen. Patient's travel to various other departments of the hospital, for scans, x – rays, that kind of thing.

I'm quite happy living in this room by myself. I enjoy privacy. And let's face it, in my current condition there's no better place to be than away from the others. I can't imagine laying on a ward, talking to Joe Smoke about his recent bowel movements or what he achieved back in the seventies. Screw that. If I'm gonna die, I'm gonna die in peace.

This morning I awoke to a visitor. Believe it or not, as I stirred, contemplating a choice of whether to stay in bed or waddle to the toilet, a familiar voice called out to me.

"Hey douche bag."

I looked across to my chair where an old friend had made himself comfortable.

"Chris? How in God's name did you get in here this early? Visiting isn't until this afternoon."

He chuckled, placing his hands behind his head. "Chris Lester, American ninja." I swung myself around on the bed, grimacing at the sharp pain that ripped through my torso. "You alright?" he asked, noticing my discomfort.

I nodded. "Yeah."

"You don't look it."

"Thanks."

"You're most welcome."

The early morning cloud in my vision impaired my sight, and a swift rub of the eyes restored it back to normality. I almost expected him to vanish after this, but he didn't. Chris sat there, clear as day. I hadn't seen him since forever, but he wore age well. Unlike me. I looked like a wrinkled old nut sack that hadn't been shaved for decades.

"How did you get in here?" I whispered, afraid of alerting anyone who might be passing the door.

Chris shifted in the chair revealing a white coat strewn across the back. If he'd warn that along with a mask, as some doctors still did after the whole Covid epidemic, he would have free access to wander around the hospital without being challenged.

"I heard you were sick. Had to come and see you, man. It's been too long."

"When was the last time. Moonshine Alley?"

"Moonshine Alley," he affirmed.

Decades. He had been absent for decades. I couldn't help but feel disappointment toward him. The time that passed had been far too great.

"So why'd you take so long? Why not get intouch sooner?"

The smile dropped from his face. "It's not easy to get out and go visiting people. No matter what you think."

My disappointment turned to confusion. "I just don't understand. After all these years?"

"It's not that I didn't want to, Callum. Once you're done, you're done. I've been away for what, fifty-two years? How was I supposed to get out of somewhere you're not supposed to get out from?"

I closed my eyes and placed a finger to my temple. The onset of a headache began to emerge. Today would not be a good one.

"Okay, well you're here now. What is it you want?"

"Callum, come on. Don't be like that."

"This is a lot for me to take in, you understand?"

"Alright. Listen, I'll give you some time and come back when your more..."

"Awake. Maybe I'll be more open once I've had a coffee and piss."

Chris stood from the chair. He nodded and made his exit, but not before halting at the door.

"Callum. No matter what you think of me right now, it's good to see you again."

I sighed. I hadn't seen him in years but we parted on good terms. That had to count for something. "It's good to see you, too."

He stepped out of my room, brimming with confidence. How the hell he had the nerve to pull a stunt like this was beyond me. It worked, though.

Not ten seconds later Marvin, my male care assistant strolled through the door.

"Good morning Mr... holy shit! You're awake?" He stepped back with false surprise.

I flipped him my middle finger. "Screw you."

I love it when Marvin is on duty. He's a small guy, shaved black hair and a black moustache that look more fluffy than whiskered. He has this vile, dark sense of humour that I love, and always manages to make me laugh. Not like the rest of them. This guy has character.

I went about my morning in the usual routine, not noticing until the early afternoon that the white coat Chris had used to break in still hung across the back of the chair.

Chapter 12: Home

"Where have you been, Callum?" Mom asked as I shuffled my saturated body into the hallway. I looked at the varnished floorboards beneath my feet, now pattered with water droplets that fell from my coat. Lonesome Jones burst into my mind. An overwhelming sense of both fear and dread washed over me.

"Camping," I replied, unable to make eye contact. His face glared at me. I'd lost control of my thoughts, and everywhere I looked I saw him.

"Why didn't you come home sooner? Dad was just about to come get you."

Aunt Penny jogged up the steps, on to the porch and into the hallway. "Sure is raining cats and dogs," she said, removing her coat. Mom closed the door as she ambled inside. I dropped my bag on the doormat.

"To what do we owe this pleasure?" Dad said, entering the hall.

Aunt Penny smiled. "I came for a drink with my brother, and a talk."

"Don't you have work to do?" Dad quipped, always one to wind her up. They exchanged a few barbs before heading into the kitchen. I remained where I stood, looking down at my feet.

"Are you okay?" Mom asked a moment later. I peered up. She frowned, not with anger, but concern.

"Yes," I replied, lying through my unbrushed teeth. I had to think quick or she'd clock that something was afoot. "I just feel, you know, cold. Like I'm coming down with something."

"Well, I'm not surprised considering how long you've spent out there in that rain. Leave your clothes here and go jump in the bath. I'll make you a coffee. Go on, now, go sort yourself out."

After she left I stripped down to my underwear, left my clothes where I stood then headed upstairs.

The bathroom just so happened to be my most despised room in the house. Functional, yes, but adorned in the most horrendous shades of pink I'd ever set my eyes upon. The bath? Pink. The vinyl floor? Chequered pink, with the odd darker shaded square here and there, making up some random pattern that I didn't much care for. The tiles around the bath shone generic shades of white. They gave a valiant attempt to break the awful colour Mom had chosen for this room, but still nothing could take away from just how overpowering the colour had become.

I popped the plug into the bath and turned on the taps. No matter what I did, or how hard I tried to focus, Lonesome Jones would not leave me. I sat in the bathwater watching steam rise from the surface. It swirled and contorted, revealing his face for a second or so before dispersing. I brushed my teeth. The condensation on the mirror formed a screaming mouth, being murdered by an unseen assailant. Me. Or Chris…

I entered the kitchen, hoping I could keep my mouth shut and not say anything that gave the game away.

"You really are looking bad," Dad told me as I joined them at the table. A cup of coffee sat there waiting, just as Mom had promised. I decided to play the illness card a while longer, in an attempt to get in my room for the rest of the day without raising suspicions. Instead of dressing in day clothes I wore my pyjamas, slippers and dressing gown. That would be the best way to emphasise my imaginary cold. Here's a tip for you, kids. You want a day off school? Wear pyjamas and a house coat the night before. Nothing says illness like pyjamas and a housecoat. You're welcome.

"So, what did you lot get up to yesterday?" Aunt Penny asked. Sitting beside a fully-fledged police officer in full uniform could not have happened at a worse time. Of all the God damned days...

"Not much," I began, peering into my coffee. "Camped. Ate hotdogs and marshmallows. Woke up this morning, packed down and came home."

"You came in at a little after two. It wouldn't take you that long to pack down your tent," Mom replied. I had to think quick.

"We didn't get out of the tent straight away. We stayed in for a lot of the morning hoping the rain would clear."

I took a sip from my drink. The warmth rippled through my body, causing goosebumps across my back for a few seconds. And that was my inquisition complete.

The family spoke about some kind of inheritance meeting that Aunt Penny had been chatting to my Dad about. A long-lost family member they could barely remember in New York had left them something. There were complications of course, as there always was in these type of situations, and throughout dinner they made a plan to clear everything up. Dad, being his own boss and able to take time out when he needed it would go with Mom to New York for a day or so that coming Friday to see what was going on and how our family had been implicated.

Me, being the lucky individual I am and who'd just become an accomplice to murder, would spend the time with Aunt Penny. Friday night would be a bit of a turd, as she would be working the four 'til midnight shift. As luck would have it, she was set to work the desk, which meant that I'd be able to stay at the station with her.

For some reason, my Mom didn't mind me camping with my friends on the outskirts of town, but being left by myself at home? That was a different story. No matter how much I explained that Dad's tools didn't bother me and that I wasn't going to mess around with them, she still had the idea that somehow I could burn down the house, cause myself some serious harm or just create chaos if left to my own devices. Anyone else suffer this kind of hypocrisy from their parents as a kid? Was it just me?

And so the plan came to be. I'd get to leave school on Friday and head to the police station where I'd be staying until midnight. I protested. I complained. I assured them I could look after myself. It all fell on deaf ears. Friday night, the accomplice to murder gets to spend an entire evening with the police in their station. Man, I might as well go to the holding cells and choose which one I wanted for the rest of my life.

Friday was going to be swell. Real swell...

I opted to spend the rest of the day in bed. I said goodbye to Aunt Penny and retired to my room. Mom and Dad checked in on me from time to time. Dad even tried to lure me down with Ed Sullivan and Bonanza on the TV, but I didn't take the bait. I just lay there, my mind replaying that scenario again and again and again. I knew Lonesome Jones had been wrong. I knew we acted to protect ourselves, but my faith that anyone would believe us if we told them just wasn't there. At some point, with all these thoughts running through my mind, I drifted off into a restless, dreamless slumber. It didn't feel long, though. Before I knew it Mom had put her head around the door to see how I felt, and tell me that it was nearly time for school.

I rose out of bed like a ghoul from the grave, and noticed that she had placed my wages on my bedside table. Lucky for me she'd checked my pockets before washing my clothes. Included in that pile of coins I noted the sparkling penny. Lonesome Jones' sparkling penny. I took a moment before opening the draw in the table. I took the coin and placed it inside before slamming it back in place, hiding the coin from the rest of the world.

Chapter 13: The Monday Blues

The Monday morning rain reflected my mood as I wandered along the sidewalk. Rain. Not hard enough to soak me through, but hard enough to make me miserable. Any other day I would do my best to avoid puddles, but today I splashed through them without a care. That despicable old hermit haunted me. My mind filled with the image of his lifeless eye staring up at me when I reached down to take his pulse. A night of sleep had not made me feel any easier. I was, in fact, terrified.

Something which also didn't help quell my nerves had been Charlie's absence on my way to school. I walked past the park where we met every morning, debated to wait a moment, but moved on. My spirit did lift a little while later though, when I found him on the steps to the main entrance of school. The idiot had been late and decided to proceed direct, knowing I'd almost be there. He also seemed off, like our actions had finally sunk in. He'd been our leader up in those woods, and probably hadn't had time to contemplate his actions.

I didn't see any of the guys that morning. I wandered from one classroom to the next, amid the hustle and bustle of kids and teachers racing to their next lesson. The world existed around me, but alone I cut a figure of withdrawal. Lonesome Jones followed wherever I walked. It had been his blank, lifeless stare after death that haunted me. I couldn't focus.

The morning took a century to pass before the bell rang to signal lunch. Again, I ambled into the cafeteria amid the mass of bodies jostling for food and seats. What hit me the most, though, was Louis. Louis always stood up on a seat or something, scouring the mass of bodies to find me. Today he didn't. That shook me. Amid the babble and hubbub of voices attacking from all directions, the lighthouse to guide me home had vanished without a trace.

After a minute or so of patrolling the tables, I found them, and for a moment I wished I hadn't. Chris looked awful. Pale, strained, he'd aged thirty years overnight. Charlie didn't look too bad, but I knew for certain he put up a front. Louis? Terrified. In fact terrified was an understatement.

As I attempted to sit down a body pushed past me, and in my seat appeared douche bag numero dos, Billy Brewster.

"Thanks for saving my seat for me, butt munch." He placed a tray of some horrendous, hardly edible shit down on the white surface. I expected Troy Peller to appear and continue with the insults, but he didn't. "So, did your friend tell you about the beating we gave him on Saturday?" Brewster asked, smiling a large, toothy grinto the rest of the Wolf Pack.

"Yeah,, he did," Chris began, "but he also said it was two on one, and that you got chased away by an old man. I wouldn't be showing off about that, you know? Not only did you double team him, an old man ran you out. Billy Brewster, representative of the wrestling team, scared away by an old barber. Think about that."

"Hey, Brewster?" I said, noticing that Peller still hadn't appeared. "Where's your master? Where's Peller?"

"Some trip. They had to leave at recess. Why? What the hell does it have to do with you?"

"So, your backup is out of school, and you decided to jump on a table with four guys and cause shit?"

At that moment, Brewster realized what I alluded to, and something happened that none of us foresaw. Without second guessing, Louis stood from his seat and grabbed Brewster's sweater, yanking him from the chair. The wrestling jock fell into the passing footfall of lunchtime kids, courtesy of the softest kid I had ever known. Gravy, vegetables and some kind of meat product sopped on to his clothes. The kids around us began laughing. Brewster wiped some gravy on to his hand, looked at it, then to Louis. *I* looked at Louis. His anxious demeanour had been replaced with aggression and conflict. My unrecognisable friend scowled, his face contorted into an expression I had never witnessed from him before.

"You gonna do something, Wee Billy?" Charlie asked, standing beside the aggressor.

Brewster looked at us. The other kids laughed. Finally, one of the school bullies had been hit back. Brewster pushed his way out of the crowd, jeered by those around him. In a matter of seconds our tormentor had vanished, leaving everyone and everything to simmer down.

"Man, I hate that kid," Louis growled, returning to his seat. I found myself fascinated by this outburst. Like I've said before, Louis was about as much use in a fight as a spatula to a plumber. The change appeared odd, but I attributed it to the act we committed the day before. Thing was, he wouldn't be the only one to undergo a significant change.

All that week, I waited for the police to announce they'd found a body in the river, or Lake Medina. I expected that the announcement would be made with a warrant for my arrest and those of my friends. Try as we might to shake the shadow of Lonesome Jones from hanging over us, we couldn't quite do it. Wherever I went Lonesome Jones followed. He peeped out from the corner of the cubicle in the school toilets. He hid behind the tree on my walk home. He stood at the bottom of my yard when the dark evenings rolled in.

Worst of all, he lived in my mind as a constant reminder for what we had done. I tried to counsel myself. I kept thinking that I had done no wrong. The selfish side of me tried to reason that my involvement had been as a victim, not an aggressor. Still, if everything went to shit and we got caught for this, I'd be as guilty as Chris simply for being there. We all would.

Louis continued an aggressive streak. I mean, not going into school and fighting kids or anything like that, but more of an intolerance. If somebody said or did something dumb he'd yell out at them, calling names and throwing insults. He even argued with Mrs Leeson in class one day after she announced to the class that he hadn't tried hard enough with his homework.

    Any other time, he'd have just sat there, dropped his head and said 'yes Mrs Leeson' during the tirade she threw at him, but this time he'd argued back. Got himself a detention in the process. I couldn't remember the last time Louis had detention. In fact, that may have been his first. The point is, Louis had become more challenging as the week wore on, which became a real concern to me, and a sign that he struggled to cope with the aftermath of what we'd done.

    Charlie lost his humour. That in itself was catastrophic. Never in my life had I known him not fire a quick one liner here, or a funny insult there. His goal had always been to amuse himself. He didn't care if you laughed along or turned away in disgust. Charlie was out to make Charlie happy. The fun-loving, mischief making kid I once knew had turned somewhat serious. The jokes were gone. He wandered the corridors with a serious tone about him. He didn't stop to talk to people, and his attention toward Erika Ricketts had all but vanished.

    A few times, I passed him on my way to lessons, and he did nothing more than offer a nod and a wink. It was so serious, in fact, that even Erika herself had noticed. One afternoon I watched as he walked past her, not uttering a word or even acknowledging her presence. And for the first time I saw her look forlorn as he wandered by, as if she missed the childish interactions he instigated. That's when she approached me about him.

"Hey, err, Callum?" she asked that afternoon as we prepared to enter class.

"Yeah?" I replied, wondering what the hell the beauty goddess would want with me.

"You're friends with Charlie, right?"

At that moment My stomach did a little somersault. I half-expected something to emerge about our evil deed.

"Uh, yeah," I said, stepping aside to let some other classmates into the room.

"Do you think he's been acting weird these past few days?"

I tried to make light of the situation and smirked a little. "It's Charlie. He's always weird."

"I know he's always weird, but, like, now he's not weird. And that's weird. Does that make sense?"

It made total sense. I knew what she was saying. My biggest concern about Charlie at that point had been realised. Other people were starting to notice his subdued persona. First Billy Brewster with Louis, and now Erika Ricketts with Charlie.

"Yeah, you make sense," I responded, trying to figure out a plausible cover up. "I don't know. We always seem to have Troy Peller on our back, and I think its wearing him down." Under the circumstances, I thought that was a good enough story.

"Yeah. Troy Peller is a real jerk. And Billy Brewster, too. Don't let them get to you, though. Just ignore them."

"That's what we try to do."

She flashed a brief smile. You know, the one that melted the heart of every heterosexual male in Pittsburgh?

"Don't tell him I asked about him, okay? I don't want him to think...well, you know?"

This reaction brought a genuine smile to my face. No matter what happened, she still had that image to uphold.

"My lips are sealed." I zipped my mouth up and crossed my chest. Erica began walking into the class. She stopped.

"Hey, Callum?" she said, looking over her shoulder.

"Yeah?"

"Stacey likes you."

I think my jaw dropped. That was not at all what I was expecting.

"What?" I asked, almost unable to comprehend what she had just said.

"Stacey. She likes you."

Erika took her seat in class. I smiled to myself. Yeah, right. Stacey likes me, huh? I didn't know much about love and relationships at that point in my life, but I did know that pretty girls like to play pranks on average boys. I took it with a pinch of salt and made my way inside. Still, I kept that smile for a while. I hadn't smiled since, well, you know?

Chapter 14: An Impromptu Sleepover

Thursday night came. I harboured some concern as Chris hadn't shown up for school since Monday. Louis had knocked for him on Wednesday just to see if he was okay but couldn't get an answer. Mom and Dad were packing for their trip away, and once they had gone I'd try to call him on the telephone. I knew the chance of contacting him would be slim, but you didn't know unless you tried.

I sat in my room drawing cartoons and listening to the rain as it rattled against the windows. I found myself dealing with my situation by drawing comic strips depicting what we had done. Of course, they didn't resemble Lonesome Jones or any of my friends, I didn't want to take the risk of someone finding them and putting two and two together. For extra security, at the top of each page I wrote 'origin story.' If a wandering eye did catch my drawings, it would look like I was creating a superhero from scratch, not reliving my past atrocities.

In the pictures I depicted Lonesome as a criminal. This happened in all my comics. What use is a superhero without a supervillain, right? The story played out with a group of police officers surrounding said Mr Jones. In the blink of an eye Lonesome attacked, and of course they put him down. One of the officers couldn't deal with the situation and became a brooding supervillain. But, I had no idea how to create a superhero to thwart him. I kept repeating the same process every time; find Lonesome, kill him, turn into a villain. Where the hell was my hero coming from?

I dropped my pencil and leant back in the chair. Every minute that passed lessened the burden of being an accomplice to murder, but still the weight hung heavy and wouldn't allow me to escape.

"Callum? Can you get that?"

"Get what, Mom?" I shouted, wondering what in hell she was asking me to do.

"The door. Someone's at the door."

Back in the 60's you could open your door at night and not feel intimidated by the world outside. Every motherfucker knew that every door to every home was left open, but standards and society conformed to a lawful way of living. During that time we were safe in most aspects of life. Kind of hard to imagine today. The 60's were the best. You find anyone old enough to remember them and they'll all tell you the same.

I wandered casually downstairs and opened the door to the outside world without a single care.

There stood Chris, clad in nothing more than a t-shirt and jeans. The poor guy trembled beneath the cold and saturated clothes that clung to his body. He contorted with sadness. His glassy eyes struggled to hold back tears.

"Jesus, Chris, what the hell have you been doing?"

"Can I come in, please?"

"Sure."

I stepped aside allowing him entry from the dank, autumnal night. By this time Mom had descended the stairs to see who had been knocking.

"Mrs Clark, I was wondering if I could stay with you tonight, please?" Chris asked. I'd never seen him so feeble.

"Oh Chris, I'm not sure. Not tonight. You see, we're very busy getting ready for our trip and..." Chris trembled, frozen to the core. Mom limped across to him. "Whatever has happened?" she asked, leading him toward the kitchen.

"I just don't want to be home," he replied.

My parents, the kindest people I ever knew, took him in as he'd asked. He had a hot bath, a meal, and even a pair of my pyjamas. My favourite pair, too. That bastard. Everyone knew that Chris' mom struggled, and my parents put it down to another of her drunken outbursts. For the first time, though, I didn't think this was the reason he appeared so broken. I believed, well, I *knew* it was something else.

We lay in the dark. Me upon my bed, Chris upon various cushions that gave him some kind of comfort from the floor. I didn't know what to say to him. Ever since that day things had changed. He was different. I was different.

"He's not dead."

"What?" I asked. His statement caught me off guard.

"Lonesome Jones. He's not dead."

"What are you talking about?" I rolled on to my side so I could peer over to him.

"I see him."

"You see him? Lonesome Jones?"

"Everywhere."

"Chris... man," I sighed. "I'm worried about you."

"No shit."

"That old bastard is dead. He's dead."

"He isn't, Callum. He's still alive. Everywhere I go. In the distance I see him watching me. Sat in class I look out the window and there he is, across the way, staring right back at me."

To say that Chris' statement was unnerving wouldn't do it justice. My nervousness resurfaced, heart beat rocketed, and breathing became nothing more than a raspy gasp.

"Is this what everything has been about? No showing school? Tonight? Coming here?"

"Being here is the only place I feel safe."

We laid in silence once more, listening to the rain outside. I thought things over in my mind. Surely Lonesome Jones being alive was a good thing, right? It meant he wasn't dead, and thus Chris hadn't murdered him. I mean, sure we'd get into trouble for beating his ass and leaving him to die, but I'd take that over a murder charge any day. As I began relaying this to Chris I noticed he had fallen asleep. It was the only time since Sunday that he hadn't looked stressed.

I awoke in the middle of the night. Thunder rumbled in the distance, rattling my bedroom floor. The rain fell heavier than when I'd fallen asleep. In the poor light I could just make out a figure standing by my curtains.

"Your awake?" Chris asked, turning to me from the window. I sighed, quelling my initial half-conscious belief that Lonesome Jones had somehow gained entry to my home.

"Yeah," I said, pushing myself up. "What are you doing?"

"He's found me."

I launched out of bed and dashed across to the window.

"Where?"

"Right down there." Chris pointed down the waterlogged street. I didn't want to look. Those butterflies awoke in my stomach once more, but I had to. I had to know for myself. I followed Chris' direction. The rain distorted my vision as it trickled and danced across the window. "On the corner." My eyes strained to see through the saturated glass. I found the corner Chris referred to, but to my relief it stood empty.

"I can't see anything."

"You can't see him? Just there?"

I strained again, peering through the rainfall, but even a second attempt couldn't convince me that anyone stood there, let alone a dead man.

"No one."

Chris moved forward, studying the area he had identified. "Your right. He's gone."

At that moment I looked at my friend with great concern. We'd all been affected by our actions in different ways, but seeing people who weren't there? That to me suggested that something psychological had happened. Unknowing what to do next, I placed a hand on his shoulder and suggested he got some rest. Soon Chris was back asleep on the makeshift bed, and I lay awake with more worries than I'd had going to sleep.

Chapter 15: Ut-Oh

The next morning my parents dropped us off at school before heading out to their meeting. I swore I wouldn't give Aunt Penny any grief during their trip away, kissed my Mom and entered the wonderful Millers Fall High School in which to learn. Chris had thanked her for allowing him to stay, and providing him with some lunch. We went through the morning as usual and caught up with Charlie and Louis at recess. The talk of the day was my visit to the police station for the night, and I swore to keep my mouth shut and head down. My ears would be open, though. Always open.

So, the end of the school day came, I left with my friends through the main entrance and found Aunt Penny parked up waiting to collect me. We wandered across to the patrol car. Penny stood leaning against the bonnet like some kind of action hero. She glanced me a smile. Not even John Wayne could lace her boots.

I loved my Aunt. She acted like the big sister I never had. She looked out for me, gave great presents at Christmas and stood up for me if the need arose. A five-year marriage had turned sour when her husband played away with a young receptionist at his work. He knew he'd done wrong, and he tried everything to reconcile, but Aunty Penny didn't take him back. Realising their marriage had ended, he moved out of state, but wouldn't sign the divorce papers she requested of him. Kind of like a big 'fuck you.' You don't want to take me back? I'll make sure you never get married. At least, that's how it looked to me. If the whole episode taught me one thing, it was to never get on my aunt's bad side. You had one chance. Once that was gone, it was gone.

"How are you doing, boys?" She asked as we approached the patrol car. We replied that we were fine. "Well, I need to take my nephew to Lake Medina straight away. Jump in."

"Why?" I asked, opening shotgun.

"Lonesome Jones has died."

I sat in the car away from the bustle of a crime scene. Vans, cars, people, suits all hustled around me. The clouds opened releasing a constant fall of rain that splattered on to the windscreen. Through the distortion I could make out the blurry shapes of professionals as they went about their business. My heart hadn't settled down from the initial shock of hearing Lonesome had been found. Chris almost collapsed. How my aunt hadn't known something was wrong I'll never know. I'd waited until Aunt Penny moved out of earshot before telling him I'd call during the night to keep him up to date about things. We had agreed to meet up at my house after I finished work the following day, where I could also explain to Charlie and Louis what I found out.

The driver's door opened bringing me back to the here and now. Penny slumped down into the vehicle clutching a notepad and pen.

"Everything alright?" I asked, doing my best to sound calm.

"Yes. We're heading back to the station. There's not much here for us to do. I gotta file these statements." She threw her notes into the back. "Can you believe it? Dog walkers found him this afternoon. Dog walkers. What idiot comes here to walk in the freezing cold, wind and rain? It's the coldest place out here."

Like I said. Dog walkers. Tough as old boots in this town.

"Is it definitely him? Lonesome Jones?" I asked. I crossed my fingers and toes hoping that there had been a misidentification.

"It's him alright. Poor sonofabitch."

God damn it. Whoever told us that crossing your fingers and toes for luck was a damn liar. I squirmed in the seat. "Why poor?"

"Well, because he's dead." Penny looked at me. "You okay, Callum?"

"Cold," I replied, right off the bat.

She smiled. "Well, let's go get you a cup of police station coffee. That's sure to warm you up."

We headed through the dismal evening to the outskirts of Millers Fall. Upon Carver Road, the main exit out, you'd find the police station halfway up an incline, looking out across town. It wasn't huge by any means, a single level building that housed a few rooms, reception area and holding cells.

I stepped through the main entrance into a waiting area decorated like an old hunting lodge.

Wooden slats adorned the walls making it cosy yet atmospheric. Turning right led to the holding cells, turning left lead you into a corridor where a couple of interrogation rooms could be found. The police officers desks were located in a larger room at the end. Sergeant Travis, a young, slim gentleman was the only officer on duty in the building at the time. He sat behind his desk scribbling some notes down in a book.

"Shouldn't you be out front on reception?" Penny asked as we entered.

Travis looked up. "I'm rushed off my feet. It's been non-stop out there," he replied with a heavy dose of sarcasm.

Penny smiled. "Good job it's me and not the sheriff."

Travis smiled back. "You will be. One day."

The police station had become something of a hangout for me when my friends were all busy or doing things with other people. I'd go and hang around with Aunt Penny if she was working reception, and became something like the station's pet over the years. Most services have a cat or a dog if they decide to own animals, Millers Fall police station had it's very own pet Callum. I used to help out, of course, tidying this, watering the plants, the menial things that no one else had time to do, all that kind of stuff. I wasn't ever a fixture up there, but it also wasn't unusual to find me volunteering around the place.

I sat at Penny's desk, drawing superheroes on a wad of paper she'd found for me to entertain myself with. The station remained quiet, no calls, no townsfolk entering to report this or that. Penny and Travis spoke about Lonesome Jones, about his way of life and how they were surprised he lasted as long as he did. The rain continued outside, rattling the windows hidden by the blinds. I had my cup of police station coffee as promised, and I swear to God that no other coffee will come close to how good it tasted.

As the hours passed, I relaxed a little. I had faith in the plan we'd carried out. It'd make complete sense for someone to sustain a head injury during a fall around a rocky area. At a little after seven Sargent Travis vacated the building, returning twenty minutes later with pizza from the local pizzeria. I sat at Penny's desk, eating more of the pizza than I should have, and drinking coffee whilst the rain fell outside. Life was almost good. Almost…

Sheriff Lewis arrived back a little before nine with a few other officers and a guy in a suit who I didn't recognise. I sat there, ignored by the law whilst they chatted about Lonesome, transporting him to the local hospital, carrying out an investigation and various other topics surrounding his death. I shifted uneasy at the mention of an investigation, but quickly settled when the guy in the suit mentioned accidental causes. I heard him mention a fall, and at that moment the weight of the world lifted from my shoulders.

The suit left to continue his work, Aunt Penny and Sargent Travis went out to another part of the station doing some work, and I remained at the desk drawing my superheroes and eating left over pizza.

"So, how are you doing Callum?" the sheriff asked as he wandered past. He took a cold slice as he settled down at a desk across the way.

"Fine, sir," I replied, shading a vampire army cadet created fresh from my mind. I looked up at the ageing Sheriff who winked at me whilst eating. "Do you know what happened to him? To Lonesome Jones?" I asked, beginning a subtle enquiry to find out what he knew.

"Well," he began, clearing his mouth of his meal, "not really sure at this point. It looks like he had a fall and sustained a few injuries. That's all we know at the moment."

"Oh," I said, trying hard to contain my smile. "You know, he was intown not so long ago? Ted offered him a haircut but he declined."

"That sounds like him alright. Never accepted any help from anyone."

"I only ever saw him once before then," I said, making conversation for the sake of doing so.

"It was very rare anyone would see him. He'd just wander down whenever he needed anything. Never disclosed where he lived. God knows where that was."

"It's a mystery," I added, knowing full well that my friends and I had discovered the area he had resided in.

"As far as we know, he lived somewhere up in the woods. Guess that's a risk in itself. It's a miracle he hasn't killed himself before now."

I nodded. "When me and my friends go camping there's always one of us coming back with some kind of injury. You know? Where we've tripped and fallen. We've come home with cuts and bruises and had no idea how we've got them. It's so easy to get a head injury if you're not careful."

"I agree with you Callum. When you're up there next, make sure you take care. It's not all happy camping. The threats are real."

"I'm about to clock off, Sheriff. I'm afraid I need to take my nephew with me."

Aunt Penny entered the office. I looked at the clock. It read midnight.

"Wow, that's gone fast," I said, standing from the table. I took my coat that hung across the back of the chair.

"You both have a good night, or what's left of it," the sheriff said to us.

"Straight to bed for him," Penny replied, picking up my school bag. "He's got work tomorrow."

"You still going into work after finishing this late?" he asked me.

"Yep. I gotta pay the bills."

After some small talk with my aunt we left the station and headed home. I did indeed head straight to bed, but still kept a conscious thought to call Chris. I knew I couldn't do it straight away, and he did, too. I laid there listening to the rain against my window. I mean, what the hell? The rain hadn't let up all week. If it didn't ease soon we'd be at risk of some serious flooding.

At two in the morning, I visited the bathroom and then opened the door to the spare room where Aunty Penny slept, and sleeping she was. Her heavy snoring confirmed this. Perhaps she dreamt of being a tractor? Perhaps this godawful battering my ears took was the reason her husband played away? Probably not, but the thought crossed my mind. I took the opportunity to head downstairs and entered the kitchen where our telephone hung beside the refrigerator. If she did awaken and came downstairs, I could hang up and claim I needed a drink. I had it all figured out. I punched in Chris' number, and within one ring he answered.

"Callum?" he said in an instant.

"Yeah it's me," I whispered.

"Oh God, man! What's going on?"

"Alright, relax. Listen, It's working. The plan is working. They think Lonesome Jones fell."

"They do?"

"Yeah. They came back to the station and said that's what they thought happened. I mean, they've got to do tests on him but they said it was an accident. He fell."

"Are you sure you're telling the truth?"

"Yes, Chris, I'm telling the truth. It was an accident. They're saying it was an accident "

I heard the relief as it expelled from his mouth. "Holy shit."

"Listen, I have to get back to bed before my aunt finds out I'm not there. Come meet me from work tomorrow and I'll explain all on the walk back to mine. And don't worry, they don't think we're involved. Now go get some sleep. You've looked like shit since all this happened."

"I've felt like it, too."

"Well stop talking to me and go rest. I'll see you tomorrow." I hung up the phone and sighed my own sigh of relief. After a moment of taking in the situation I returned upstairs to bed, and slept through until Aunt Penny woke me up for work the next day.

Chapter 16: A Visit at Work

The rain continued into Saturday, but I walked with a little spring in my step. After the hell I'd been through the past week I finally started to feel a little like my old self. All singing, all dancing. And better. A lot better.

I arrived at Ted's with a smile on my face, one which increased after I'd found he'd already purchased a coffee for me. The rain seemed to put people off that day, but I didn't care. I was too wrapped up in my own happiness to wonder how much money Ted would take. We had a few gentlemen in an out in drabs, but it wasn't really a bustling day like I expected.

By mid-afternoon, we bid farewell to what I guessed would be our last customer, but as always there was still time for one more to pay a visit to the barber's chair. I had taken hold of the brush and swept around the corners and nooks, trying in vainto catch the hairs that decided to hide there. Corners were the worst. If hair got nestled in them, it became like drawing Excalibur from the stone; almost impossible. The bell above the door rang, and I turned to see Sheriff Lewis stroll in. It took me by surprise for a second, but I smiled and greeted him.

"Hello Sheriff."

He removed his hat to reveal the thick mop of grey hair I'd seen only yesterday. He nodded and smiled.

"Hello yourself, Callum. How are you?"

I smiled once more. "Great. Just great." And I believed it, too.

"About time you had that cut," Ted quipped as he entered from the back rooms.

Lewis chuckled. "Time, my friend. It's having the time to do it."

The sheriff removed his standard leather jacket revealing casuals, not uniform. Ted spun the crimson barber's chair around.

"Off duty today then?"

"Supposed to be," Lewis said as he placed his frame down on the leather seat. "Not today though. I got called in."

"Lonesome Jones?"

Sheriff Lewis nodded as Ted spun him around to face the mirror. "You heard about it, then?"

"Yep. Nothing travels faster than gossip and bad news in this town. What are we going with? Short back and sides?"

"Whatever I usually have."

Ted chuckled. "It's been so long I can't remember your usual."

"Just make it tidy."

Ted sprayed some water across his hair, then with a comb and scissors began cutting. He placed the comb through the hair, lifted slightly and snipped the tops away. I finished sweeping, placed the brush in the small store cupboard and returned to the shop floor. I made work for myself by tidying the counters.

"So, anything you can tell me about Lonesome?" Ted asked as he continued his work.

"Nothing much to tell. Just paperwork. Coroner believes his death was accidental."

Hidden from view I smiled.

Ted nodded. "Well, can't say as I'm surprised. Living the way he did something was bound to happen sooner or later."

I moved over to the waiting area, sat down on the couch and tidied up some papers.

"Open and shut," the sheriff began. "State's taking over his affairs. Having no family and no assets should make it quick and easy to deal with."

I looked up at the mirror. My eyes met Sheriff Lewis. I became unnerved for a second before shifting my gaze back down to the papers. My heart rate increased. My gut told me something I wanted to ignore. It told me something was wrong.

For the rest of his haircut the sheriff spoke to Ted about sports, news, politics, the usual crap you chat when in the same situation. I swear Ted had the exact same conversation with customers earlier in the day. Twenty minutes later the cut had been finished, making the law man appear ten years younger.

"I'll have to grab some change from the back," Ted said after taking the fee for the haircut. "Won't be a moment."

Ted vanished from the shop floor. I pottered around, making myself as useful as I could.

"Callum, I wanted to have a quick chat with you," came the sheriff's voice.

I turned to face him. My blood pressure increased.

"Okay."

"Something's been chipping away at me since last night. You know, this whole Lonesome Jones thing we got going on? When we were in the station, you said to me you thought that anyone could sustain a head injury up in the woods. Remember?"

"Yeah?"

"I just... I wonder how you knew that? You know, the head injury? That was a detail no one knew, except for myself and the coroner. At least, not until the report came back this morning confirming it. I wanted to ask you how you heard about it?"

My body seared with adrenalin. Butterflies flurried en mass throughout my body. I'd fucked up big time and had to think fast to make a plausible excuse.

"I didn't. I was just speaking, like, you know? It's easy to get a sprain, a bone break or a head injury while your hiking. Falling can cause a whole load of injuries if you're not careful. That's what I was talking about. This one time, Charlie Beaumont took a knock on the head while we were camping up there. He had concussion for a week." This statement at least was true. Charlie did bang his head running into a thick, low reaching branch one time we were fooling around in those woods.

Sheriff Lewis nodded. "Okay. That makes sense. So, you were just speaking generally?"

"Uh, yeah. Just remembered that time was all."

He nodded. "Gotcha."

"There you are," Ted began, emerging at the perfect moment to break the conversation. He placed a few coins in Lewis' open hand. "Brand new. Look at the shine on those." Almost like the penny that sat in my dresser back home, I thought.

"They should be worth more in this condition."

Ted shrugged. "Maybe in a few years' time?"

The sheriff smiled and bid his farewells. As he exited the shop he turned to me. "And you're right, Callum. It can be so easy to hurt yourself in the woods. You take care, now."

I watched through the window as he disappeared into the rainfall. I'd managed to come up with a great cover story in a nanosecond that didn't incriminate either myself or my friends. Take a bow, Callum, take a bow. Still, the sense of unease lingered.

I stepped out on to the sidewalk and into the dreary, overcast evening. The rain rattled my coat as its relentless downpour ceased to give in. The street itself stood empty, except for a passing car that hissed like a viper through the surface water as it glided by. As I began my journey home my eye caught a trio of rain coats approaching me. As they drew closer I saw that they belonged to my friends. My stomach dropped at the sight of them wandering toward me. We were scheduled to meet up later on that evening. I had only arranged to meet Chris on the walk home, so I knew something was up when I recognised them.

"Callum," He called as I came into earshot.

"What's up?"

"We're heading back to Moonshine Alley," Charlie replied.

"What? Why are you going there?"

"I don't know, man," Chris said, still appearing stressed. "Just something ain't right."

"I told you, there's nothing to worry about. It's been ruled accidental."

"Chris told us," Charlie said.

"I ain't never been so relieved in all my life," Louis added.

Chris grimaced. "It's not that, I... I don't know what it is. I just feel like I need to go there."

"I can't, guys," I began as the rain fell upon us. "My Aunt is expecting me. she'll lose her shit if I'm not home, and that means I'll be grounded when my parents get back."

"Come on," Chris sighed. "We won't be long. Half an hour? Forty-five minutes?"

I closed my eyes and sighed.

At least the three of them had the foresight to each bring a flashlight on this little adventure. Dragging me into the wilderness against my will had irked me to a tremendous level, but I could see, as did Charlie and Louis, that Chris wasn't firing on all cylinders. Something troubled him.

Chris used his flashlight first once we got into the treeline. He wandered a few feet ahead with

Louis, leaving myself and Charlie to follow not far behind. The rain brought with it a chill as it fell. Mix that with the autumnal wind that whipped between the trees, and you get an idea at how cold I had become.

"He's not right," Charlie said to me in a low voice.

"Chris?"

"Yeah."

I agreed. He'd not been the same since...

"Why did you guys agree to do this?" I asked, lowering my voice so Chris wouldn't hear.

"For him. He's wound up about it. He's just so desperate to get up here."

"Why?"

Charlie shook his head. "I don't know."

We trudged through the darkness guided by Chris' solitary light. I hoped to God that the other flashlights would work when needed, otherwise we'd be in for a long, cold night in a now foreboding woodland. Rain rattled the leaves around us as we pushed on. The lush scent of pine filled my nose, released into the air by the element pounding them from the clouds. Soon Chris' light found Old Man's Claw, and he stopped.

"What is it?" Louis asked, coming to rest beside him. Chris cocked his head.

"Rayburn Point."

"What about it?"

Chris pursed his lips together. "Something."

I stood in the rain, shivering as the wind danced about me. I worried that the Chris I once knew had withered away, leaving this anxious, dishevelled shell of a kid in his place. Chris shone the flashlight toward the entrance to our camping ground.

"It's not Moonshine Alley I need to go to," he told us. "It's there. Right in there."

Charlie sighed. "Look, man. Are you sure its the right place? How do you know?"

Chris turned back to him. "I do. I just know."

I flashed a glance toward Louis. His confused expression mirrored mine in the poor light.

"If we're going, we need to go now," Louis said. "It's already after dark, which means my hide has an appointment with a leather belt."

Chris nodded. Without saying a word he turned back to the ferns and pushed through. One by one we followed.

The river screamed past us, its power maximised due to the heavy rainfall. We stood in the clearing. Memories of our last camping trip flooded through my mind. The tent, the camp fire, sitting eating hotdogs and drinking beer, sharing a cup of hot water with Louis.

Chris stepped toward the cliff edge and adopted the same pose he had on the trail just a few minutes before. His head cocked to the side, as though catching the sound of a whispering voice. He stood there for a minute or so, taking in the surrounding as the woodland spoke to him.

"Chris. What's going on?" Charlie asked, stepping forward into the clearing. "What's all this about?"

Chris turned to face us. The flashlight illuminated him in a strange and uncomfortable light. He grasped his dad's ring, something I'd never seen him do. He clasped it like a lucky charm, like it was something that would protect him.

"He's still here."

We stood silent. Louis looked to me and shook his head.

"Who?" Charlie asked, holding his arms out to the side. "Who's here?"

"Lonesome Jones."

Charlie's head dropped. "Chris, he's dead. Lonesome Jones is dead. We killed him."

"No you didn't!" Chris snapped. "I did. I killed him. At least I thought I did."

"You did," Charlie replied in a gentler tone. "Lonesome Jones is gone, and he's never coming back."

"But he's here. Can't you feel that? It's like I can feel his presence. Like a spirit. Like a ghost."

I shuddered. To my right an anxious Louis withdrew a hunting knife from his pocket.

"Where the hell did you get that?" I asked, astounded by the blade he just unsheathed.

"My dad's hunting knife. I wasn't coming up here without some kind of protection."

"Shut up!" Chris shouted, ending our conversation in an instant. Our focus came back to moment, and the realisation that Chris had finally lost his mind.

Charlie remained sympathetic in his tone. "Come on, man. It's late... it's dark... we need to be home, all of us."

Chris looked past us. His expression changed. "Someone else is up here, too."

My eyes widened. I felt it. That feeling that someone is staring at you from somewhere unseen. The river crashed past, roaring like an angered lion. The odd drops of rain pattered on my clothing. As I stood in that moment I felt eyes baring down upon me. I turned to inspect the tree line in the darkness.

"Do you see something?" Louis asked. He shone his flashlight into the trees, moving left to right then back again.

"No, but I do feel it," I replied. And I did, too. Never before had I experienced such a strange sensation.

"It's okay," Louis said, waving his blade back and forth. "No one is going to mess with us. Not while I have this."

I stood silent, smothered in the woodland's darkness as I watched the flashlight scour each and every darkened nook the area had to offer. No one appeared. No person, no animal, not even a goddamned moth. As much as it felt otherwise, we stood alone.

"Guys, we need to go. Whatever mystery is happening out here we can chase tomorrow. Right now we're cold, wet and I'm hungry. Let's call it a day."

Charlie spoke sense. We were freezing our asses off and soaked to the bone. You didn't need to ask me twice, and you probably didn't need to ask Louis a second time, either. This whole expedition settled on Chris. If he wanted to stay we wouldn't leave him alone. He knew that, because of the bond we all shared. Leave no man behind. The Wolf Pack. We wouldn't break that, not for anyone. Chris appeared conflicted. Whatever motivated him to venture up here had not been resolved. Something still troubled him, but on this occasion he let it go.

"Alright. Let's get back before you get into too much trouble."

The long walk home was not so bad. We stepped out of Rayburn Point, back to the trail and everything just kind of lifted. The tension vanished. The seriousness dispersed. But for me it was the sense of those eyes watching me. Whatever was in that woodland with us back there had decided to stay there. Out on the trail, back into Millers Fall and then back home, those eyes didn't follow.

"Can you wait a minute, Cal?" Chris asked as we entered the town. Charlie and Louis had no intention of waiting around, so they left us standing in the pouring rain. Chris removed the twine from around his neck and handed me his dad's ring.

"What's this?" I asked.

"Please. Hold it for me for a while? I have this feeling that I'm going to lose it, and I don't want to do that."

"Chris I'm not sure..."

He grasped my hand and slapped the ring into my palm.

"Please, man. I'll take it back. I just... you're the most careful person I know. Just for a few days."

I could place the ring in my dresser draw, right beside that shiny penny. It wouldn't be a concern. Chris had become so wound up and anxious about it that I could do nothing else but agree.

"Alright. A few days though. Just until you get yourself sorted out."

"Thanks, man."

Chris turned and dashed through the rain, leaving me with his most prized possession.

Chapter 17: A Strange Encounter

Having a loud, verbal dressing down is never a nice experience when you're a kid. You just stand there and take it. It's not like being an adult when you can give a piece of your mind back to your aggressor, tell them they're full of shit and walk away. No, as a youngster you just take what's given to you or feel the back of someone's hand. I didn't expect that from Aunt Penny, though. Yes, she was annoyed I'd stayed out a full hour and a half after finishing work. Yes, she lost her cool and shouted me down as I stood in sodden clothes, unable to remove them due to the verbal pounding she hit me with, but she did cool down when I told her it was to spend time with Chris in an attempt to cool him down. After a bath and some dinner I sat with her and decided to explain a few things about my recent activities. Not everything, of course, but more my concern for my friend.

Aunt Penny, ever the wise, explained to me her thoughts on the situation. Millers Fall was a small community back then. Everyone knew everyone, which meant everyone knew everything about you. In some instances, they knew about your problems even before you did. Penny explained to me that it was Chris' family life she felt was having a negative impact on him. I mean, I've written it down here a few times already. His dad serving in Vietnam, his mom turning to the bottle. And now add to that the fact he murdered a guy, and something's going to give sooner rather than later.

So the chat finished, I watched '*The Wolf Man*' on TV with a cup of coffee and then took myself to bed with the evenings events swirling in my head.

I lay there in the darkness listening to the rain outside. Chris, Charlie, Louis, Sheriff Lewis, Lonesome Jones, they all swirled in my mind. I closed my eyes and bore down upon the lifeless corpse of Lonesome Jones, murdered by a strike to the head. Chris popped in there. I saw him struggling. I saw how much stress he had endured. I wondered why he'd been so adamant that I took his dad's ring, which I'd placed beside me in the draw. His mind had gone, that was for certain. He needed professional help, but the danger of revealing what we had done threatened to surface if he started talking to someone. This thing was never going to go away.

In one sense, I wished everyone knew what we did, as at least it could be over and we wouldn't have to keep such a huge secret to ourselves. I dozed as all these thoughts dawned upon me. Somewhere in the darkness Lonesome Jones laughed, and told me he'd see me soon. Whether that was in my mind or in the real world, I couldn't tell.

The debris of the woodland floor cracked and shifted beneath my bare feet as I headed toward Rayburn Point. I walked barefoot, which for me was unusual, but there was no discomfort or pain as I ambled between the trees. An owl hooted off in the distance, and the river ran by at its natural tempo. The sunlight bore a plethora of vibrant stars, all visible during a clear, midday sky. They twinkled and flashed, no longer bound by a night-time darkness.

Something was wrong.

I entered the clearing. A fire burned in the pit of stones we had built on our last camp out. The logs were there too, and upon them sat Chris, Louis and Charlie. They turned to me as I entered from the tree line.

"We've been waiting for you," Charlie said, patting the space next to him on the bark. I wandered over and sat myself down.

"Sorry. I don't know what I was doing."

"Well your here now," Chris replied. That's when I felt something different. Chris sat in no more than a grey vest and dark underwear. Louis wore a traditional white pyjama set with blue trim. Charlie bore a red t-shirt and black pyjama pants. I looked down. I sat there in my full pyjama outfit.

"Anyone know what's going on?" Louis asked.

"I gotta be dreaming," I replied.

Chris shuffled on the log opposite. "If it's your dream, Callum, you better tell us why we're here."

"It's not his dream. It's mine," a voice came from the trees. I turned to its direction but found myself paralysed. No matter how much I fought, there was no way that I could move. The rest of the guys sat in the same position as me. Straight back, head forwards. We'd been cursed.

From the shadows emerged the horrifying corpse of Lonesome Jones. Only he wasn't a corpse. He was alive. His flesh sagged blue where he'd been exposed to the river for a prolonged period.

Lonesome reached down to the fire and opened his palms.

"Warmth. I've missed this." Water dropped from his fingers. "It's been so cold where I've been. So cold." The bloated corpse turned his attention toward us. We grimaced. and struggled, to no avail. There was nothing we could do. Trapped like rats. "You know why you're here?" he asked. The pale, swollen body of our victim, still clad in his camouflage fatigues stumbled toward us. I fought as hard as I could, attempting to break free of my invisible shackles and sprint away from the clearing. Fear clutched me tight.

Lonesome Jones sat down on a stone. Water seared from his mouth and jacket, splashing on to the debris. The smell of stagnation accompanied the liquid as it poured out.

"Do you believe in ghosts? Life after death, that kind of thing?" Up until last week I only believed it possible inside a comic book. Lonesome smirked. "It's all true. Maybe not how your lead to believe, but it's real. Look at me." Our heads turned in his direction. He raised pale palms. "Boo. That's right, I'm a spirit. Not a ghost. Do you boys know the difference between them? Ghosts and spirits? Let me tell you. A ghost is an apparition that doesn't interact with the environment around it. It just occurs. Like a memory. Won't look at you, won't communicate with you. Just walks its path and vanishes. That's a ghost. Now, a spirit is different; it's aware. It can interact with its surroundings and communicate with the living if it wishes to. Throw things around. Bump. Bang. That's a spirit. That's me. You know why I'm a spirit? I'll tell you. Because you bastard's killed me."

Lonesome's demeanour turned to anger. The swollen skin around his mouth contorted into a scowl.

"My life may not have meant much to you, but I was happy. I lived in peace out here in the wilderness, amongst nature, amongst these trees..." He trailed off in thought for a moment, lost and sorrowful. "Do you know what it's like living here? It's the most wonderful, beautiful experience you could ever wish for. Waking up to the smell of pine. Bathing in the cool waters of a flowing river. Your music is the sound of the wind flowing through the leaves. Your friends are the wildlife you hear foraging deep in the woodland. But best of all it's the peace you exist in. No hustle and bustle of the world rushing around you. No need to spend all your day at work or school. Just mother nature and yourself existing in harmony… I miss it. I miss it so much..."

At that moment, I felt true regret at what we'd done. Until this point I'd focused on hiding away the truth to save us all, and worried about the change in personality Chris had undergone. I'd never considered Lonesome Jones at all in this predicament, not until now. As I looked at the bloated, waterlogged corpse we'd damned to walk the earth I empathised with him, and I was truly, truly sorry for what we had done.

Lonesome stood up.

"Here's my warning to you all... I'm coming for you, and you'll be the first, Christopher. You won't see me. You won't know I'm there until your final moments. It may not be now, next month, next year, or even during the next decade, but sooner or later I'll come calling for you, and for your debt to be repaid. Now you'll know the torment that I am damned to. Knowing that I come for your souls but not knowing when I will collect them is far more tormenting than killing you now."

A breeze picked up through Rayburn Point. It ruffled our clothes and battered the fire's flame.

The rough surface of log changed into something more comfortable. The diminished firelight vanished leaving me in darkness. I opened my eyes. The breeze flowed in through my bedroom window. I sat up. Somehow, I'd returned home.

Chapter 18: Taken

The next morning, I awoke with an odd sensation that something was off. You know? We all have that feeling from time to time. You can't put your finger on it, you just sense that something isn't what it should be.

I lay in bed gathering my senses whilst my groin screamed for me to take a piss. I didn't want to get out of bed, and I was going to leave it as long as I could before I took the necessary trip to the bathroom.

I recalled the dream from last night as I lay there in discomfort. It felt so vivid, and for a moment I believed it may have been real. The power of the mind. It does have an effect on you, no matter if you believe it or not. I dismissed my subconscious, rolled out of bed and did everything I had to do.

Sundays were lazy days. I loved milling around in comfortable, baggy clothes just doing my own thing. Sometimes I'd meet up with the guys, sometimes I wouldn't. Today I didn't want to see them. Nothing against them, of course, I just wanted to shower and drink coffee. Besides, the rain continued outside, and I didn't enjoy the thought of biking to someone's house in the rain that the damn clown continued to throw at me.

The day passed without any hiccups. I took my shower, wore my clothes, played some vinyl's and drew some pictures. My parents arrived back during the early afternoon, freeing Aunt Penny to take at least part of the day for herself before she returned to the beat the following day. She hadn't mentioned anything about my after-work activities that would have grounded me for certain, even though it wouldn't have bothered me in my current mood. I didn't want to get an ear bashing from my folks, though, so I was grateful to my aunt for that.

Mom and Dad told me about their meeting, which bored the shit out of me. Turns out we weren't in receipt of a million dollars. After that I switched off. By the expression on Mom's face it bored the shit out of her too, but Dad was very excited. He'd been left a small property out of Long Island. God bless that guy. Only he could become that excited about a dishevelled house needing a fortune to renovate. Mom decided to cook a fine meal to celebrate us being together once again, but fifty-four years later I can't recall what she served. I do remember what happened during that meal, though. Something shook my entire world.

"Aunt Penny told us about Lonesome Jones," Dad said as we conversed around the table.

"She said she had to take you to scene for a while?"

That uneasy feeling surfaced again. "Yeah. I stayed in the car though. Didn't see or hear anything."

"That guy was a legend. Shame, really."

I lowered my eyes. "Yeah."

The phone rang. "I'll get it," Mom stated, jumping from the table.

"So what you got planned this week?" Dad asked. He always like to have an idea of my schedule, even though it never changed from one week to the next.

"Same as usual. Go to school, come home. Work on Saturday."

"Saturday is going to be busy for you. Ted will have you putting up the Halloween decorations I'd imagine. You trick or treating this year?"

"Yes, sir."

"You not getting to old for that?"

I smiled. "No, sir. I'm trick or treating forever. You can't stop me."

Dad grimaced. "Your such a kid."

Mom returned to the table and sat down. By her expression I knew something was wrong.

"What is it," Dad asked, getting there before I did.

She sighed and reached over, grabbing my hand. "Callum, I'm so, so sorry."

My heart sank. "What is it?"

"It's Chris… he's dead."

Chapter 19: Back to Reality

"Mr Clark, how are you today?"

I awoke to a beeping monitor. Dull daylight crawled between the blinds from outside. Marvin stood beside me with a tray of food.

I turned my head to him. "I'm dying, Marv."

"Yes you are my friend, but that doesn't mean you can't enjoy eggs and bacon for breakfast."

I smiled. This guy was the best carer in the hospital bar none.

"Don't beat around the bush, just tell it as it is," I replied.

He smiled back. "Hey, Honest Marv. That's what they call me."

"They call you a lot of other things too, I can tell you that."

Marv placed the tray on my table. "Now, will you eat this yourself or do I gotta sit here and give it to you?"

"I'm perfectly capable of feeding myself."

"I know. But *will* you feed yourself? That's the question."

Marv took hold of the bed remote and began to raise my upper body. The system hummed as it pushed me forward. He moved the table closer, removed the plastic cover concealing my meal and presented me with the worst eggs and bacon I'd ever seen.

"You trying to kill me faster with this?" I quipped.

"Mr Clark, you're blocking this bed. The sooner your dead the better. Now come on, eat your breakfast. You want a coffee?"

"Is it as bad as the food?"

"It won't extend your life, but it won't kill you either."

"Don't suppose I can get you to run out and bring a coffee in for me, eh?"

"Ha. You see this, Mr Clark?" Marv pointed to his butt. "They're shoving a mop up here so I can clean the floors as I walk. Unfortunately you make do with hospital beverages."

I assessed my breakfast in detail. Rubber looking eggs. Looked like there was a piece of shell in there too. And the bacon? Hell, you could replace the sole on your shoes with that.

"Alright. I'll have one. But I'm going to complain about it all day." I took the knife and fork from the table's surface.

Marv smiled. "Okay, I'll get your coffee for you." He left my room, leaving me to deliberate what part of the shoe I should eat first; the sole or the rubber. Within a moment he returned, placing a steaming hot cup on the table.

"There you go sir, weak and black, just how you like it."

"That's impressive. You remember."

"That's because I'm a legendary assistant, Mr Clark. But do me a favour, though. Eat your food. You need to keep your energy up."

"It doesn't matter how much I eat, I'm still gonna die in here."

"Maybe. But I want you around as long as possible. You make it worth my while coming to work every day."

I looked at him. This guy who had been a stranger when I first arrived had since become the closest thing to family outside of my own family.

"I'll be back to collect your empty plate, Mr Clark. And I'll check under your pillow and bed if you decide to hide it. So don't bother. Enjoy."

And with that the whirlwind left, leaving me with the monotonous tone of the monitors keeping me company.

Chapter 20: Getting into Trouble

The rain fell heavier the following day. Flood warnings had been issued on the local radio and TV channels. The sky rolled with dark, dark clouds. I took it as a sign. The sky was mourning, as was I. I hadn't slept. I hadn't eaten. I hadn't done anything. The pain in my heart weighed me down. With each step my legs ached. I hurt. Everything hurt. My sail had been unfurled. My drive had stopped. Nothing mattered to me anymore. Nothing.

Mom had attempted to keep me home. She didn't think it was a good idea for me to be in school that day. I thought otherwise. If I stayed home I'd have too much time to think about things and I wanted the distraction.

I walked to school in the downpour, battered by the rain as it crashed down upon me. I focused on the sidewalk, stepping through puddles in a dream-like trance. I wanted to wake up and for all of this to be a nightmare.

I waited at the bench for Charlie. The rain fell that hard I couldn't see across the park. I waited longer than I should have, uncaring that I'd be late, and not caring what the punishment would be. I kind of knew he'd head straight to school with the weather being this bad, but I used it as an excuse to loiter for a while.

So, I did indeed arrive late, entered my class late and ignored the teacher. It wasn't until recess when things livened me up.

I strolled through the doors and into the bustle of kids eating their lunch. I moves slow, wandering through treacle as the mass of multicoloured bodies zoomed around me. I didn't know what I was doing. My autopilot kicked in and I wandered to the table we often frequented. Amongst the chatter and chaos I found my friends. They both sat looking as solemn as I felt. I sat down opposite them. Charlie sat with the usual plate of school slop he had become accustomed to. Louis didn't even have his lunch.

"Did you hear?" Louis asked.

I nodded. "Yeah."

I couldn't bring myself to look at them. That's where it hit me, sat in that hall with the other kids laughing and joking around us. The four of us always ate together. Not one school day had passed where we hadn't, unless one of us had been off school for any reason. We sat together at the table. Not four any more, but three. Three of us, and it felt horrendous. My eyes stung as I held back the emerging tears.

Louis sighed a long, hurtful sigh. "You know what happened?"

I shook my head, still unable to look up.

"Suicide," Charlie said before taking a drink of his milkshake. "His mom found him in the bath. One of his dad's old razorblades was hanging around and, well, you can guess what he did." Charlie swiped an imaginary razor across his wrists.

"Jesus," I sighed, struggling to come to terms with it. "Why? Why would he do it, though? I don't understand?"

"He wasn't right," Louis added. "He hadn't been right for a while. Ever since..."

We sat in silence, listening to the crowds of kids chattering around us. Three kids looking solemn as hell. Three kids who should have another sat beside them.

A pair of hands slammed down on the table.

"Look at you three miserable douche bags." Troy Peller grinned his arrogant, better-than-you grin. Billy Brewster of course stood behind him, never far away from his lord and saviour.

Troy ruffled Louis' hair. "What's the matter? Your boyfriend off school today? Is that why your all looking like a slapped ass?"

Louis looked at Charlie. Charlie looked at Louis. In an instant Peller stumbled back, smashed in the face with a tray that Charlie had launched. Louis jumped up, smashing the athletic body of our buffed tormentor. Charlie, the thinker that he is, hit Brewster with a mean looking right, knocking him to the floor and taking him out of the game. Louis bore down on Peller, relentless with his punches.

A crowd began to gather. Kids shouted and screamed around us. Charlie threw some harsh kicks into Peller's side, Louis stomped down upon him. No remorse, no cognition. Just anger. Pure anger. They'd turned feral, kicking the ever-loving shit out of our long-term tormentor. Peller screamed. Mr Mathers the English teacher stormed over, pushing kids out of his way like a boat crashing through the waves. He pulled them both from the melee and marched them from the scene.

I gasped. Peller had been destroyed. He lay there with blood seeping from his nose. An eye had swollen and it looked like his nose broken. Still conscious, Peller grasped his ribs. Sickened and afraid, my anxiety increased when he began crying. The school nurse had been informed, and she rushed over to assist him. I stood up, unable to process what had just happened. Louis and Charlie? For real? I looked at the battered face of the wrestling captain, and God you'd have thought he'd been chomping on a hand grenade. Brewster had a stream of blood pouring from his mouth. As I watched the whole thing unfold, I showed little remorse. Those two asshole's deserved it.

The Principle, Mr Tanner, had always been a fair man, at least in my experience. I hadn't had that much to do with him since I started school, but no meeting or encounter between us had ever been drawn from my behaviour or lack of academic prowess. In fact, the only real time I'd ever spent with him had been when teachers were sick, and he'd covered their lessons.

I sat in his office alongside Mom, staring out the blinds into the constant rainfall. I watched as the rest of the kids left school for the day. I didn't. I was in the principal's office with a parent, which meant I was also in a world of shit. This meeting was different, though. Beside Mom sat Louis and his father, and beside them Charlie and his mom. From the expression Mr Johnson bore, I knew for sure he'd be dishing out another belt whooping on their return home. Charlie's mom appeared worried more than anything else. My Mom? Curious I'd say. She knew something was wrong for sure. Me? I was pissed. I was more than pissed. I was livid. I knew this meeting had been called after the beating Troy Peller took, and sitting there knowing I had nothing to do with it boiled my blood. Louis and Charlie were my friends and they'd let me down.

    Principal Tanner strolled in, apologising for the delay. Behind him Sheriff Lewis appeared. I rolled my eyes and turned back. I couldn't shake this man for anything. Everywhere I went he appeared. The sheriff closed the door as Tanner walked around to the desk to his chair.

    "What have you been doing?" Mom whispered to me. I shrugged my shoulders.

    "Sorry for the delay ladies and gentlemen," Tanner said as he sat down. "This isn't usual for me to conduct a meeting like this, but considering the circumstances I feel it appropriate."

    "Can you tell us what this is all about?" Louis' dad asked.

    Tanner leant back in his chair. "Any of you boys want to explain what happened today?" I looked at my feet. I had no intention of telling anyone anything. The room remained silent, save for the kids outside leaving into the dreary afternoon.

    "Okay, I'll tell you what happened," Principal Tanner began. "There was an incident in the cafeteria today. These three gentlemen were involved in a fight. Well, not a fight. A beating. Two students have been injured. One seriously. These three boys inflicted said injuries. They beat up two of their fellow students."

"What?" my Mom blurted. "That doesn't seem like the sort of thing these boys would do?"

"Unfortunately it is the truth, isn't it boys?"

"Yes," came Charlie's muted voice.

"Yes," Louis whispered. I remained silent.

"How bad?" Louis dad asked.

"Bad enough," Tanner responded. "One student has a split lip and is missing tooth which he's receiving treatment for. The other is not so good."

"The other has a concussion. He also has a broken nose, hairline fracture to his cheek bone and severe bruising on the right side of his body," Sheriff Lewis added.

"It was Peller's fault! He started it!" Louis snapped.

"Wait. You guys beat up Troy Peller?" Charlie's mom asked.

"Yes we did," Charlie began, "and he deserved it."

"The fact of the matter is this," Principal Tanner said, bringing their attention back to the situation, "Troy Peller is in Hospital being treated for the injuries sustained by these three boys. And as I have it, he may have to undergo observations overnight."

"Christ," Mom said, looking to the ceiling.

Sheriff Lewis made his way around to the desk. "I know you boys have been hit with real bad news. I know it's going to take a toll on you, but you can't behave like this. You've broken the law, and seriously too. Troy Peller's parents want to throw the book at you. And they have a case. Witnesses saw you doing it. Lots of them. We're not talking a slap on the wrist here. If your all charged you will go to court, and you will go to jail."

"We're too young for prison," Charlie quipped.

Lewis grimaced. "Don't cut wise with me, son."

Charlie took a slap around the head, courtesy of his mom. "Shut up!" she added, then nudged him to make her point.

"Hey look, I gotta say something," Louis added. "It was Charlie and me. Callum had nothing to do with it."

Charlie nodded. "He's right. Callum did nothing. It was all on us. You can't punish him for something we did. It isn't fair."

"Is this true?" Mom asked me.

I nodded, and then decided to speak. "I sat there. I watched them. I'm still to blame, because I could have got them to stop. I could have stopped them and I didn't."

"What happens now?" Louis dad asked. Tanner looked to Sheriff Lewis and gestured for him to speak.

"Let's not beat around the bush. We all know Troy Peller is not a nice kid. Once I explained to his parents that his list of crimes and misdemeanours would surface if they took this further, they cooled off. They're not pressing charges."

"Thank God," Charlie's mom sighed.

Lewis stood straight. "In my mind there's nothing for you to answer for. Seems your luck is in for now. School-wise? Well, that's up to the principle."

Our focus returned to Principal Tanner. "In this case Callum can continue as normal. I'm sorry to drag you into this. However, for you two, it's a different story." For the first time in the meeting I looked across to my friends. "You're both suspended."

Charlie's mom sighed.

"How long for?" Mr Johnson asked.

"Until I know what do with them."

"You're not thinking of expelling them, are you?"

"I'm not sure. Not yet."

Our parents stayed behind in the office whilst the three of us waited in the corridor.

"I don't believe it," Louis began, huffing and puffing with disdain. "Suspended. Man, my dad is gonna tan my hide when we get home."

"Don't worry about it," Charlie replied. "We get a few days off school. Make the most of it."

"But what if we end up expelled?"

Charlie smirked. "They're not gonna do that. Troy Peller has done far worse than we have. The sheriff even told us so. If they won't expel him, they won't expel us."

Louis nodded. "Well, at least you're okay, Callum."

His words stabbed me. They cut me deeper than his hunting knife could ever penetrate.

"What do you mean I'm okay? Are you fucking stupid? You two just beat the shit out of the biggest bully in the school and you think I'm gonna be okay? Peller will be back. Brewster will be there, with the entire god damn wrestling team. I've now got to get through school with a bullseye on my back because of you two. What help do you think you've been to me? Just get lost. Both of you. I don't want to be around you anymore."

I turned and stormed the corridor, pushed the entrance doors open with excessive force and stepped into the rain. There I stood awaiting my Mom. I didn't care that I was wet. I didn't care that I was cold. I wanted to be as far away from those two assholes as I could get. I wandered down the steps to a small bench where kids often sat awaiting their pickup at the end of the day. I slumped down, not caring that my butt splashed into surface water resting upon the surface. I cussed and swore to myself, enraged that this situation had occurred. The thought of attending school by myself didn't fill me with confidence. I'd become vulnerable, and for the first time in my educational life I felt it. Charlie and Louis, those god damn idiots.

"You okay?" a familiar voice asked. I jumped from my thoughts to see I'd been joined by the Millers Fall saviour, Sheriff Lewis.

"Yes," I sighed, hoping he'd accept my answer and move on. He didn't though. He remained beside me. I sighed again, unable to comprehend the hand I'd been dealt with at that current moment in time.

"You seem to be in the thick of it at the moment, Callum. Bad things happen wherever you go."

"Like what?" I asked, annoyed at what he alluded to.

"Well, Troy Peller gets beaten up. Your there but not involved. Second, I still can't figure out how you knew about the injuries Lonesome Jones sustained when his body washed up in Lake Medina."

At this point I'd lost the fear factor attached to the murder. I'd become angry and incensed at everything that happened afterwards. Angry at Louis, angry at Charlie, even angry at Chris if I'm being honest. My life appeared to be falling apart thanks to Chris' actions and the cover up we'd created for him. It had become tiring. I wasn't in the mood for this shit. Not anymore.

"I told you, Sheriff. It was just a thought. I've seen head injuries happen up in those woods. That's just what I thought about when we were talking."

The sheriff nodded, pursing his lips together and raising his eyebrows. "Well, it doesn't matter, now. The case has been closed. Lonesome Jones' death has been ruled accidental. The report says he died due to injuries sustained during a fall. No one can argue with it. It's done." I didn't engage in any further conversation. This bastard was on to me, of that I had no doubt. "But I just wanted to let you know something. I'm keeping this case on the back burner. I'm not writing it off. I know for certain there are people around who know exactly what happened to that crazy old guy up there in the woods. One day those people are gonna slip up, and I'm damn well gonna be there when that happens."

Mom exited the school doors into the rain. She stood a moment, almost perplexed that the sheriff and I were having a conversation. He looked to her then back to me, tipped his hat and said goodbye.

Fuck that guy. He didn't have a leg to stand on. We'd gotten away with it. We'd gotten away with murder. Charlie's plan had worked.

That evening, Mom explained to Dad what had happened. He reassured me, and somehow managed to subdue some of the anger still surging throughout my being. I still felt pissed off with the whole Troy Peller episode and having to face school with Billy Brewster watching my every move, though. Dad expressed concern about Charlie and Louis, and their recent behaviour, but I assured him that the emotion of recent event's had gotten the better of them. As the evening wore on my anger toward them eased, and I recalled everything we'd been through together so far. By the time I crawled into bed my attitude changed. I empathised with them and felt bad about what I said back in the corridor.

I wouldn't see them again until Chris' funeral. That's when I'd tell them I was sorry.

Chapter 21: Coffee Call

"Hey. Hey! Mr Clark. Wake up!"

I stirred, opening my eyes to an early summer morning. Gold light streamed in through my window, a stark contrast from the overcast mornings I had been used to. I moved on the creaky bed, looking in the direction the voice came from. Marvin poked his head through the door into my room.

"Is it time for you already?" I asked.

"No. I've just got in, but I brought you this." Marvin showed me a take-out coffee cup. "I got you one. So at least you can have a decent coffee to start the day." He strolled in and placed it on my bedside table, beside my notebooks and pens, and removed the lid.

"You're a good man," I said.

He smirked. "Remember that in your will."

"Asshole."

He chuckled. "Alright. I gotta go get the scrubs on. I'll be by later on to give you a hand. Enjoy your drink."

He left the room as swiftly as he had entered. I took a sip of the coffee. Liquid heaven. Head and shoulders above anything served in these four walls. Care assistants don't get enough credit for their work. He really went above and beyond just so I could have a coffee. Salt of the earth that guy, and all care support workers, too. Salt of the earth.

Chapter 22: Saying Goodbye

The day of Chris' funeral reflect the mood of the occasion. Clouds and moderate rain fell during the late October morning. I'd never been to a funeral before, and that caused me anxiety in itself. Add to that the fact it was one of my best friends, and, well, you can guess how nervous I became. I hadn't slept well during the night. Various images haunted my mind, keeping me awake and unable to relax.

I conjured horrendous thoughts as I lay there, like Chris rising from the grave as some kind of demon, chasing the three of us down, ready to exact his revenge because we didn't help him when he needed it. I tossed and turned, and at 3 o'clock decided to give in and lay awake. This backfired as my anxiety now held hands with exhaustion. Not a great combination.

I stood in my bedroom folding my tie into a windsor. That rain pattered against the window, and I hoped it eased by the time of the service. I didn't see the point in having a tie as I'd be wearing a dark jumper, but Mom insisted. A knock at the door stalled my concentration as Dad walked in, himself looking immaculate in a dark suit.

"You okay with that?" he asked, gesturing to the tie.

"Fine."

He sighed, wandered over to my bed and sat down.

"You know, you haven't really spoken much about all this," he said, looking everywhere in my room except to me.

"There's nothing much to say."

"Come on, Callum, it's not just this. You've been acting strange for a while, now. Your more reclusive, you're getting into fights at school..."

"I didn't get into any fights!" I snapped. My anger resurged, but I kept my cool. Today of all days I didn't want to argue.

"Okay, but you know what I mean? I'm worried about you, and so is Mom."

"I told you, I'm fine." At that moment, I noticed the Windsor unravel. I grabbed the tie and threw it across the room. My head had gone. I didn't know what to do or what I felt. I stood still, looking aimless at my mirrored reflection. At that moment a hand rested on my shoulder. I turned to my Dad. Lonesome Jones, Chris, murder, death, everything crashed down upon me in an instant and I buckled. My lip trembled. Tears trickled from my eyes. Dad hugged me, pulling me tight.

I don't know how long I stood there. A second? A minute? An hour? The embrace was one of love, and everything I carried seared out with my tears. At that moment I returned to the fourteen year-old kid, I'd been before all this happened, and realised a hell of a lot had been resting on my shoulders, probably more so than any other fourteen year-old in the world at that time.

As my cries subsided Dad took a hold of my shoulders and looked me in the eye.

"Today is going to be a tough day, I'm not going to lie. You shouldn't have to experience the death of a friend at your age. But know I'm here for you, as is Mom. As bad as this is, you'll come out a stronger person. Things won't ever be the same, there just becomes a new normal. But you'll get through it. It may take some time, but you will. And if you need anything at all, just talk to me."

He pulled me close and hugged me once more.

"I love you, Dad."

"I love you too, pal. Now come on, let's get this done. Tonight, when it's all over, we'll both have a beer. Just don't tell your Mom."

The service took place way out of town. Chris' mom had a family connection to Evans City. Her family were resting together in a cemetery out there, and she'd decided this is where Chris should lay, too.

I sat in the car watching the rain against the windows. I didn't know how long we had been driving, and I didn't care. I just wanted everything to be over. The cemetery itself stood faded and bleak as we entered. Lower down in a small valley a cluster of leave-less trees huddled together. We turned left at a fork in the road and passed by a small building stood isolated to our right. A shed that belonged to the grounds keeper of the cemetery, maybe? Tiny flags bearing the stars and stripes flapped in the breeze beside their owners graves. Gnarly branches reached out from the trunks on which they belonged, seemingly reaching for help as we passed them by. The further we ventured into the cemetery the darker it became. It took on an atmosphere by itself, one of foreboding, and upon my exit of the car a sense of unease emerged.

People had gathered on a small hill, all clad in black, all mourning the loss of a youngster.

The first person I laid eyes on was Charlie. He'd ventured out with his mom to get there. Louis was also due to attend, but in the cluster of bodies I didn't notice him.

"I want to see Charlie," I told my parents as we walked across the sodden grass.

"Yeah. Of course," Dad replied, clutching Mom's hand to steady her as they navigated the terrain. She could still be unsteady on her feet at times, especially in these conditions.

I left them behind and wandered across to my friend. He bore a brown cardigan, white shirt and black tie beneath a simple jacket. It was the first time I can recall him dressing up. His trousers had been pressed and even in the rain, I noticed his shoes shine.

"Hey," I said, walking up to him.

"Hey," he replied softly. His face bore a solemn expression, one that reflected the days event. At that point I felt even worse than I had before about shouting at him and Louis, and I wanted to apologise right away.

"Look, I'm sorry for sounding off at you guys back at school. I just...I don't know what I was thinking."

Charlie didn't reply. He just placed a hand on my shoulder and smiled. His eyes turned glassy and welled with tears. My eyes prickled and a tear escaped down my cheek. Charlie pulled me in and we shared an embrace. This kind of thing was not the general practice for two fourteen year-old boys. It wasn't cool to show your emotions, but at this point I don't think either of us cared. We embraced as the rain fell, sharing each other's grief for both ourselves and our lost friend. That's when it hit home. Chris was gone, like, really gone, and he was never coming back. Never.

"Hey guys." Louis approached, his eyes cascading already. Charlie held out an arm and he took hold of us. Louis sobbed with our arms around him. This in turn made me cry. Only Charlie managed to hold back his emotion, but even he couldn't hold back a rogue tear.

We wandered across to the graveside where chairs had been laid out, and Chris' coffin sat ready to be lowered. I looked back at my parents. Mom had cried already, but I guessed it was due to my friends and I. The coffin itself was the generic wooden choice I expected it to be. It reminded me of something you'd see in the background of Chilly Billy Cardille's *Chiller Theatre,* but it reflect the nature of the person inside. Plain and simple. Nothing dramatic.

The service itself felt hurried. The weather had a big part to play in that. Chris' mom sat on a chair looking out into the distance the whole time. Not once did her gaze shift. The three of us stood together, of course, as did our parents. By the time things had started I'd managed to pull myself together, but Louis still snivelled here and there. I looked around to see if Chris' dad had managed to come home, but it appeared he hadn't. I knew that, though. The truth, to me at least, was that his father was dead as well. I hoped that somehow they had found each other in the afterlife, something that I now believed in.

The majority of the time I spent looking at the grass. Not looking at the coffin ahead of me, and trying my hardest not to imagine my friend laying inside it.

"Hey," Louis dad said as we wandered back to the cars. "I've been speaking to your parents and we thought about heading back and grabbing a bite to eat at Doris' place. What do you think?"

I'd been so overwhelmed by the day that I hadn't paid attention to how hungry I had become. It was a sure fire yes from me, and from the other guys, too.

We sat in a booth next to the window, watching the rain rattle against it from outside. I studied the headlights of passing cars, trying to see the volume in which the rain fell. It was heavy. Damn heavy. Flood warnings were still in place across our local area. A few roads across town had been submerged, but nothing affected my route to school. The park intown had turned to a mass of waterlogged puddles and mud. Grass had all but disappeared, except for a few rogue clumps sticking up out of the rain water here and there.

It was like I had been sitting in the very front row of that circus, watching the clowns do their thing. I'd watched confetti seer into the air from one bucket, and unlucky for me I'd be the recipient of the water launched from the other. This time it wasn't just a bucket that drenched me, it was an ocean. I've said it before and I'll say it again. That goddamned clown.

Our parents sat a few tables away which gave Louis, Charlie and I an opportunity to speak freely, something we hadn't done in a while.

Charlie leant back on his seat. "The weird thing is, I was kinda expecting something like this," he began, his tone suggesting a story was on its way. "The night before this happened I had a dream, and we were all there, at Rayburn Point. I remember it because we were sat on logs but couldn't move."

My stomach rolled. "And Lonesome Jones appeared. He was all bloated from being in the river. He sat down and spoke to us," I replied. An expression of disbelief emerged on Charlie's face.

"He said it may not be today, tomorrow, next month or next year, but sooner or later he'd make us pay for what we did." Louis recalled the warning in my dream exactly as it happened. There was no way this could happen. No way.

"This is bullshit," I said, taking a french fry from my plate and shoving it in my mouth. "There's no way we could all have the same dream. It's impossible."

Charlie shook his head. "It can't be bullshit. We all know what happened."

"I'm telling you, there's no way that can happen."

"Damn it Callum, think about this! There's no other explanation. We had the same dream, or we shared the same dream."

I sighed. This kind of talk was the last thing I needed now. Premonitions, paranormal or whatever you want to call it were not a hot topic of discussion after a funeral.

"It was real," Charlie added, lowering his voice. He leant across the table. "It was real."

"There's one major problem with this," Louis began, his voice tinged with concern. "If the dream was real, it means Lonesome Jones is real. And if he's real, that means Chris wasn't crazy after all."

Charlie's eyes widened. "And he got to Chris first. Exactly like he said."

I took a sip of my soda. "Let's say that I believe you both on this. If he *is* real, what do we do? One of us is gonna be next."

Charlie shook his head. "I don't know? You're the comic book reader. What do you think?"

I had no idea. I didn't quite believe it myself, but I couldn't explain the shared dream situation. No matter what my thoughts were, I couldn't provide a plausible theory on how we knew what happened within our unconscious minds.

"Do you think he's a ghost or something?" Louis asked. "I mean, he's dead, right?"

"A spirit. that's what he said," Charlie stated.

"Then how the hell do we get rid of a spirit?" I responded.

Charlie shrugged his shoulders. "I have no idea. But you do believe us, don't you Callum?"

"I don't have any other choice."

"Okay. This is what we do." Charlie beckoned for us to lean in. "We find out what we can about ghosts, spirits or whatever the hell they are, but we can't ask our parents to help us. They might get suspicious."

"How are we gonna find this shit out on our own?" Louis asked. A light bulb flashed inside my mind.

"You two are both suspended, right? Then go to the library. Go and see what you can find out there. They have to have something, even if it's just one page in one book."

Charlie jumped in. "Callum, I've never been to the library in my entire life. My parents will know something's up if I go there."

"Then feed them some excuse about going somewhere else. Come on, man. If you two are both right, it could save our lives."

"What are you gonna do?" Louis asked me.

"I'll go to school and see what I can find out. I'll see if I can chat with Miss Wincott. She loves all this kind of stuff. I'll tell her I'm drawing a comic or something and I'm looking for advice."

Chapter 23: Talking Spooks

Miss Wincott, the expert on all things spooky also happened to be our music teacher. In all honesty you could tell this by the way she dressed. Long blouses, multicoloured scarf's, pink glasses, pendants and other strange and weird items hanging from her neck. Yes, she was that one. Curly red hair and a slim figure made her the focal point for most of the school's male population, myself included. She was a wild child, a rebel, but had the sweetest heart you could ever imagine. I don't think she had any trouble with any student at Millers Fall High School, at least not during my tenure there. The best teachers make their subject fascinating to study, and during my studies she'd gage my attention enough to play twinkle, twinkle, little star on a standard six string.

Rumour had it she'd attended the Sky River Rock Festival a month or so ago, which was a badge of honour amongst the kids at school. It placed her in the upper echelons of school legend, and cemented her status as one of, if not *the* best teacher in the establishment. I also heard she liked to dance with Mary Jane on a regular basis. That did not surprise me at all.

I'd remained vigilant during recess whilst on my own. I ate my lunch at a different table and remained out of view of the wrestling team, and in particular Billy Brewster. Troy Peller would be back soon enough, and that's when shit would really go south, but in the meantime I managed to lay low and avoid any confrontation with those that wished ill of me. During this period of isolation I hid in the school library. I did that because I knew there'd be no chance in hell that they'd set foot in there. Miss Wincott's class sat just down the corridor from the library, and I planned to dash over and ask her advice without being seen.

I trotted along the empty hallway, looking back to see if Brewster had found me. Mr Cuminski the janitor had a mop in hand and muttered as he cleaned some mess by the lockers. A trend had started where kids spilled juice around the cafeteria, thinking it hilarious that the poor old guy had to clean up after them. This had now spread out into the hallways and other areas with high footfall. That guy must have spent hours mopping up juice, water and anything else the kids could get their hands on. Still, I guess it had to be expected. I imagined him acting like a disturbed neighbour, chasing children from his property whilst waving his fist in the air if he ever caught the culprits. Poor guy.

I came to the music room door and knocked four times.

"Come in?" came a perplexed answer. I entered to find Miss Wincott sat at her table, looking to me with great curiosity.

"Miss Wincott," I began, closing the door behind me. "I was wondering...Well, I need your help...I think?" Her unwavering beauty distracted me to the point of confusion. She smiled.

"And how can I help you?"

I wandered across to her desk, nervous and mesmerised in equal measures. Some guy would be very happy hanging from her arm. That guy would be one lucky asshole.

"Um...I'm writing an essay, for homework." At that point I didn't want to say comic book. I didn't want to give her the impression I was a nerd. You never knew. Maybe once I graduated she'd take an interest in me. The chances of that happening sat between slim and none, but I wanted to present myself as masculine as I could. No comic books here. No Universal horror movies, and certainly no howling at the sky with your friends. Jesus, could you imagine anything more childish?

"And this essay is...well...it's about ghosts. I've heard you mention this kind of stuff from time to time, ghosts that is, so I thought I'd ask you a question about it...them, I mean?"

Miss Wincott smiled but frowned at the same time, confused and likely intrigued by the fourteen year-old kid taking a sudden interest in the paranormal. "Okay, take a seat."

She gestured to the chair and I sat down, forgetting the satchel hanging from my back. After an embarrassing moment of struggling to remove it I took to the seat without any further incident.

"Miss Wincott," I began, attempting to sound factual and all grown up, "I have surmised a lot about ghosts in my homework, but there's one question I need to know; how does someone get rid of one if it's tormenting them?"

Miss Wincott placed her papers down. "That's an intriguing question. I guess you start at the beginning. You'd need to know more about the paranormal before you can answer that."

"Okay. What can you tell me about it, then?"

She rolled her eyes upwards, as though accessing a long-forgotten memory. "First, if your being haunted by a troublesome energy it's not a ghost you have, it's a spirit."

"They're not the same?" I enquired. Of course, Lonesome Jones had stated this already in our shared dream, but I listened to what she said so as not to come across presumptuous.

She shook her head. "No. The best way to describe a ghost is like a memory being played back. It appears, does its thing and disappears. You can't communicate with it. It doesn't know your there. It appears and vanishes no matter what happens. A spirit is different. It's conscious of itself and of you. It can communicate in one way or another, and affect the environment around it. Like, for example, banging on walls or using a Ouija board."

"Miss Wincott, what about dealing with evil spirits? Why are they evil and can they be removed?"

"A spirit reflects the nature of the person they were in life. If someone's a bad person in life they'll continue to be so once they pass over. Sometimes, though, things can happen that turn them bad. You know what I mean? They can die a tragic or unjust way. That's why most spirits stick around, they feel sorrow at an injustice they've experienced. But removing them? Well, you could invite a priest to bless the house or person being haunted. You could also ask the spirit directly to stop haunting you, but you'd need something that belonged to that spirit during life. Having an object that belonged to them gives both yourself and the spirit a direct connection. Tell them that it's not their time any more. Most of them don't know they're dead and sometimes require to be told. That can do the trick. Also, you can call upon your guardian angel for protection. If you believe in spirits you have to believe in guardian angels, right? Even the vilest of spirits will be banished in the presence of an angel's light."

"How do people do that?" I enquired. Guardian angels were not my speciality.

"Just ask them. Close your eyes and speak with them in your mind. Reach out. Ask for help."

With nothing else to ask, well, not knowing anything else to ask I should say, I thanked Miss Wincott and left her to the pile of papers I'd distracted her from. Her input had been most useful, I just wasn't sure I believed it. Could you really banish a spirit just by telling it to leave? There was only one way we were going to find out. I recalled the shiny penny hiding away in my bedroom, the one I found in the clearing. I recalled not knowing why I took it, but hindsight suggested a premonition or something. Did I know I'd need it? Is that why I kept it all along?

Miss Wincott did ask to read my essay once it had been completed, though. That was a shit. I'd created more work for myself than I needed to. Damn it.

I left the room and flung my satchel over my shoulder. Angels? Spirits? Priests? Blessings? I'd be damned if I knew what to do with this information. I'd have to sit and go through everything she told me to see if I could make sense of it all. It would take time, and time was something we didn't have.

I crashed into the painted brick wall, chest first. My vision distorted as I tumbled around, and upon gaining my composure found myself nose to nose with Billy Brewster.

"Hey dipshit," he said, revealing a missing tooth as he barked at me. "Looks like your friends are missing once again."

"There seems to be a pattern here," I began, resigned to the fact that I'd receive an ass-whooping any second. "Do you always beat people up when they're vulnerable?"

"No. I'm here to warn you. Troy's out of hospital, and he's pissed. You're the first one he's gonna pay a visit to."

"Peller ain't shit. He got his ass handed to him by the weakest kid in school. He's riding on his reputation, and that's about to get smashed. He ain't nothing. Not anymore."

"You keep telling yourself that," Brewster replied, pushing his hands against me with greater force. "He's gonna do the same to you as you all did to him. And I'm gonna stand there and laugh at you while he's beating your brains out."

"You do that. And when everyone asks why there's a huge fucking gap in your teeth, you can tell them Charlie Beaumont knocked out a tooth."

He drew back a fist and smashed me in the stomach, knocking the wind from my lungs and crumpling me over.

"I'm not gonna beat you up. I'll let Troy do that. When he's finished, though, if there's anything left I'm gonna stomp my boots all over you." He slapped my head and walked away. The same blunt pain I'd suffered back in the alley re-emerged. I watched Brewster leave through the desolate hall, awaiting the return of his best friend.

Chapter 24: What Now?

I met the guys down at Doris' after school. I headed straight there knowing they'd be waiting for me, and I kind of hoped they had something more about ghosts and other things that went bump in the night. I had no doubt that the information Miss Wincott gave me would be correct, but I felt that attempting to banish an evil spirit with nothing more than a penny and prayer would be like attacking a platoon of Vietcong with a military grade peashooter. We couldn't drag a priest into protect us, that was for sure. Not only would our credibility be called to question, but we'd also have to explain why we needed such assistance. Sticking to one untruth had been difficult enough, trying to remember two would be impossible.

'Daydream Believer' by the Monkees played out on the hidden radio when I entered the diner. Some other kids from school sat at the counter with their milkshakes, no doubt quicker to leave school than I had been. Mr Watkins, the guy who owned the workshop where Charlie's dad worked, sat in a booth eating eggs and ham. Judging by the state of his overalls I'd say he'd had a busy day. A couple of old timers drinking their coffee chatted about the war, and just around the corner next to the window Charlie and Louis sat on opposite sides of a table, awaiting my arrival.

"Hey," I said, removing my satchel and slipping in next to Louis. "Any luck today?"

I expected the worst but hoped for the best. I didn't have a whole lot of faith in Louis researching something outside of his interests, even if he did put his full commitment and attention to it. Charlie on the other hand could do anything he put his mind to. But considering he'd never once stepped inside the town library I didn't hold out much hope. He all but confirmed this to me seconds later.

"Nah, not a thing." He reached to a tall glass housing half a chocolate milkshake and sucked the straw. "Nothing in there. No ghosts, no aliens, no nothing. Except Charles Dickens. I could give you four ghosts from '*A Christmas Carol*,' that's it."

I sighed, but expected this outcome none the less. Millers Fall was a shitty little town in the deepest recess of rural Pennsylvania. Text books and research into the paranormal just wouldn't exist within its borders.

"What are we going to do?" Louis asked. His demeanour had become one of concern, almost like the kid I had known before all of this crap took place. "I don't want to be haunted. I don't want this hanging over me."

"None of us do," I replied. Somehow the idea Miss Wincott explained to me made sense. Maybe Lonesome Jones needed that nudge in the right direction, and in doing so could find peace? If we facilitated the spirit crossing to the other side maybe everything would stop? At this stage it became the only viable option we had.

I explained my chat with the hippy teacher. My two friends listened with intent, like a pair of preschoolers listening to a fairytale.

"Where are we gonna find him?" Charlie asked, after I explained my plan to banish the evil that haunted the three of us.

I dropped my voice to a whisper. "The place where this began. Moonshine Alley."

Louis slumped back. "I don't know, guys. That place was scary enough before all this happened. I don't think I can face it again."

"Callum's right," Charlie said spinning the base of his glass on the table's surface. "That's where we found him. That's where he'll be."

Louis grimaced. "Guys..."

"We don't have a choice, Louis!" I snapped a little at my friend. In my mind this was the only option we had to eliminate the curse that attached itself to us all. I sighed and scratched my head in frustration. "Look, we have to give it a shot. We can't live like this, expecting shit to happen at any given moment. We have to try, if nothing else."

"And if we're wrong?"

Charlie answered Louis before I could respond. "We ain't gonna be much worse than we are now. We do it. Tonight. You both okay with that?"

We agreed. Another late night, another ass whooping for Louis, no doubt. His butt had been spanked so often this past week it must have hurt just sitting there at the table. It'd be worth it, though. If this stupid plan worked it'd be worth it.

What I didn't know at the time was the presence of someone in the booth behind us, listening to every single word we said. This person would also have a part to play in the evening's events. It had been by a stroke of luck on his behalf that he'd decided to call into the diner on the way home.

That person was Billy Brewster.

Chapter 25: Returning to Moonshine Alley

We hung at Charlie's house for the first part. I'd told Mom and Dad I'd be spending the evening there, settling any uncomfortable questions that may have arisen. I took the penny from my bedside dresser, and placed Chris' necklace around my neck. For luck, I thought. It was just a matter of choosing the right time to go. We were apprehensive for sure. Even afraid. Up until a few days ago, we'd thought ghosts and spirits only appeared in the late-night movies. Yes, we'd heard stories but never considered they might be real.

Lucky for us, our parents hadn't grounded Louis or Charlie for their suspension. The general line of thought had been that Troy Peller pushed one button too many and gotten what he deserved. It doesn't happen very often, but when kids and parents agree on something there's often a sense of harmony between them. We all enjoyed the togetherness of the moment, and this in turn allowed my friends and I to breach their trust and continue our shenanigans out in the woodland. I felt somewhat bad for lying to my parents after they stood by me, but hey? When you have to rid yourself of an evil spirit, you do whatever it takes.

At Charlie's place, we gave the story of heading back to my house, covering all bases and ensuring free access to roam wherever we wanted. As the last light of the early evening dwindled we took our flashlights and headed back to the place where it all started. Moonshine Alley.

The rain had eased earlier in the day. The circus clown appeared tired of messing with me. Instead a gusting wind emerged. It attacked us sporadically as we wandered to the outskirts of town. Our wardrobe had been seasonal, with both myself and Louis wrapped up in winter coats and thick trousers. Charlie remained draped in that green jacket he wore everywhere. Nothing would change that.

We entered the trail leading to Old Man's Claw. I swear as soon as we stepped on to the woodland debris the sounds of life diminished. No longer could we hear the vehicles or bustle back intown. The silence around us broke only when the wind breezed throughout the trees.

We remained quiet and cautious. I lost count the amount of times I'd been camping here and never felt worried. This time my anxiety rocketed, taking flight like an aeroplane soaring into the clouds.

"What's that?" Louis gasped, coming to a standstill in the darkness.

Charlie shone the flashlight in his direction. "What?"

"Up there. I saw it. A light or something?"

Louis pointed up ahead. Charlie turned and scoured the area with the vibrant shine from his hand. Blips of round, yellow light flickered on and off within the darkness. They flittered and flew, surrounding us from all directions. These tiny orbs of light danced in all directions, emerging from the trees and descending from the canopies.

"Fireflies," I said, mesmerised by the light show illuminating the woodland.

"No way," Charlie snapped. "They shouldn't be around now. They should be hibernating."

"There's still a few around," Louis stated. We watched as the insects omitted their light. At that moment a thought crossed my mind.

"He knows we're coming."

"What?" Charlie asked.

"Lonesome Jones. He knows what we're doing. You remember that time when we ventured here with Chris? He kept saying he could feel a presence, like he was all around or something? I've got it, now. That same feeling."

Now, up until we murdered Lonesome Jones I'd never been afraid of the woods. Cautious, yes, uneasy at times, but never afraid. Rayburn Point had been a home away from home for us, and nothing I'd experienced to that point had ever frightened me. No wildlife rustling in the darkness late at night, no owls hooting from the canopy above, not a thing. Not until we ventured there the last time with Chris. Now that I had a better understanding of the paranormal, well, a brief flirtation with a knowledgeable person to be exact, my anxiety heightened further. As I stood watching the fireflies fade into the darkness, my belief in ghosts and spirits became certain. The light show from insects that shouldn't be there, an overwhelming sensation of dread and fear, it had to be true. All of it. Nothing had made feel that way before in my life. Nothing.

"I'm not going to lie. I think we should turn back," Louis began. Charlie shone the flashlight toward him. I'd never seen the poor kid so terrified in all the years I'd known him. His lips trembled as he spoke, shivering as though an invisible snowstorm clasped him with an iron grip. Hard to believe this kid kicked three shades of shit out of our school's alpha male.

"We can't, man," I replied, utilising the softest tone I could muster.

"But we need help. We need an adult."

"We already told you!" Charlie snapped. His aggressive streak returned. I sensed his anger bore from fear, not frustration like usual. "We get an adult then everything we did will come out. If we do this by ourselves we can put it to bed and no one knows anything."

"But what if we don't do it?" Louis retorted. "What if we fail?"

"Then we don't have to live the rest of our lives afraid. Because we'll all be dead."

"Guys, come on!" I replied, unable to control my anger. Why, at this point in our mission, did they have to bicker? I pulled Charlie into my left, Louis my right and put an arm around them both. "We need to be together on this, right? No arguing, no backing out, we need to keep going. I'm not going to lie to you, I'm afraid. I'm so scared about what we're gonna find in Moonshine Alley, but one thing's for sure; tonight is the only night

I'm gonna be afraid. Whatever happens, when that sun rises this will be over, one way or another. And look at it like this; if Lonesome Jones sent those fireflies to bug us out and make us scared, he has to be trying to keep us away. If he's trying to keep us away, maybe what we've planned might just work."

"You're right, Callum. Louis, did you hear that? He has a point. We need to stop being afraid, because that damn spirit is afraid of us."

Motivation appeared in Charlie's expression. Louis nodded. Not only had I talked these guys around, but I'd settled my own anxiety in the process. Without uttering a single word we disbanded from the embrace and continued our journey through the foreboding trees to Moonshine Alley.

Chapter 26: Almost Time

I awakened into a strange but relaxed atmosphere. The usual hustle and bustle of the ward behind my closed door seemed far less busy than usual. I rubbed my eyes and found that my cloudy sight had been replaced with clear vision for the first time since I don't know when. The curtains had been opened, and in through the window beamed a brilliant, bronze sunshine, unlike anything I'd seen before. I laid there, enjoying the glow of this warm, clean light and noticed something odd. The machine I'd been hooked up to sat dormant to my side. I checked my arm and all the tubes placed inside had now been removed. I was used to the doctors poking and prodding me with various appliances, taking blood samples, all that good stuff, but they always gained consent.

    Finding myself treatment free, even if only for a minute or so, confused me somewhat. I pushed myself up on to my elbows, bracing for the pain that would rip through my body, but nothing happened. I sat upright, free, easy and without the terrible sensation of ripping myself in half. I felt great. I felt amazing. The treatment must have worked. I hadn't felt this good since my early twenties. The door swung open and a familiar voice greeted me.

    "Hey? Ass master. What you doing in here?" Charlie entered my room, as brazen and confident as ever. The only problem I had was the fact he couldn't be a day older than fourteen, and exactly as

I remember him during the Lonesome Jones hell we went through.

"Charlie?" I asked, more amazed than confused. "Is that you?" I swung my legs around and sat on the edge of the bed. Charlie plumped down and placed an arm across my shoulders.

"Do you know anyone else in the world that looks like me? Like, exactly like me, huh?"

"No."

"Then who the hell else do you think I am?"

"I don't know? I mean, what's going on? Is this another one of those shared dreams we have?"

Charlie grinned that huge shit eating smile that stretched across his face.

"Well, if it isn't, how'd you explain this?"

My mouth dropped. Both Chris and Louis entered my room looking fantastic, happy, and again back in their teens. They greeted me, slapped my back, the usual. Nostalgia washed over me and for a moment it felt like we'd travelled back to 1968 with our lives stretched out in front of us.

"What are you all doing here?" I asked, amazed and overwhelmed at the same time.

Chris smiled. "Come on. We'll show you." He gestured for me to leave the room.

"What? I can't do that. I'm sick. The doctors will kill me if I leave here."

"What doctors?" Charlie asked. Again he smiled, but this time it was the I-know-better-than-you-smile we've all experienced from someone at one point or another.

Not understanding what the hell was happening, I leapt from the bed to the door and peered out into the corridor. Just down the way to the left the nurses station sat empty. The bronze sunlight beamed in through the exterior windows, painting the hall in a calm, peaceful light.

"No one here," Louis grinned.

"Guys? What..."

I stopped. My hands looked different. The liver spots had gone, and my skin appeared taught over my knuckles. I noticed too that my apron had vanished, and I stood in the same t-shirt and jeans I wore the day I left Ted's Barbers to go camping. In a frenzy I rushed to the bathroom and peered to the mirror. Fourteen year-old me with the floppy, brown hair peered back. His expression of shock mirrored mine. I turned back to my friends, all still amused at my overreaction.

"What's happening?"

Chris chuckled. "Come on." He held a hand out to me, and without a hesitation I took hold of it. He lead me through the door, into the corridor and let go. "Ah, shit. Don't forget. My ring, right? You still have my ring?"

It took me a moment to clear my thoughts. "Yeah. In my drawer." I rushed back inside to the bedside cabinet, withdrew the drawer and took the ring Chris had asked for. I dashed back and gave it to him.

"I can't believe you kept it this long," he said to me.

"What did you think I was gonna do with it? Throw it away?"

He smiled and placed a grateful hand on my shoulder. "We need to do something."

In an instant we'd left the room, but not just the room, the hospital. The shoes that had appeared on my feet just moments before now thudded on to grass as I ran through a mass of trees and foliage, following my friends. We screamed. We laughed. We howled. Wolf Pack forever. I came to an abrupt halt, finding myself stood beside the river at Rayburn Point. The river thrashed past, spewing mist into the bright, bronze sunshine, more beautiful and majestic than I had ever seen it. Chris stood with a clenched fist. He looked down, almost afraid to reveal the ring inside. After an age, his fingers opened, and the ring twinkled in the vibrant light. He looked to the river, and with one swift movement tossed his most prized possession into the raging waters.

"Why'd you do that?" I asked. Any other time I'd have attempted to stop him, but this felt different. I didn't sense the need to.

"That ring," he began, turning to face me directly, "has been holding me back. It's been holding you back. You spent your entire life keeping it for me because you couldn't bear to lose it."

"You saw all that?"

"Yeah, I did. I visited you many times without you noticing, as I did with Charlie, Louis, and my mom. You guys were family. You still are. I had to take that ring and get rid of it, for you."

"Me?"

"Yes, for you."

"Why me, though?"

"It gave you a purpose you didn't need. It kept you going. You don't need to do that anymore."

My confusion changed to realisation. I knew why I was there. Why I was fourteen, and why my best friends had taken me back to Rayburn Point.

"This is it," I said, my voice no more than a whisper.

"But it's everything we were told it was," Louis began. "Every year that passes remains the same. You never age. You celebrate the good stuff. You go home. You go to school. You remain happy. You always remain happy."

A sensation grew inside me, one I cannot explain. A sense of happiness, overwhelming happiness fused with peace and optimism. I looked forward to the new adventure.

"You know, I kinda expect Mom and Dad to come for me at this point," I said, recalling my thoughts during the illness.

"Happiest time of your life. Who'd you love being with?" Charlie asked. That was an easy question.

"You guys."

Chris held out his hand. "Come on. It's time. Let's go see them."

I reached out as I had back in the hospital room, but the thought of my notebook sitting on the table flashed through my mind. I pulled back. Chris tilted his head and smiled in confusion.

"What's up, Callum?"

I shook my head. "I can't. Not yet. I have something that needs to be finished."

"Like what?" Charlie quipped. "Your dying in a bed."

"Let him speak," Louis requested. Charlie stopped.

"Just give me one day. One last day. Let me finish what I'm doing and then I'll come with you."

"Is that even allowed?" Charlie asked.

Chris nodded. "Of course. Remember, everyone crosses of their own free will. Once they get to this stage no one wants to return. Except you, Callum Clark." He smiled. "You are the most logical, factual, headstrong person I ever met. If you say something needs to be finished, well, it needs to be finished. Go and do it. And we'll come back when you're ready."

As he spoke these words he placed a palm on my chest. I fell back. I tumbled from an edge, falling with speed into an unknown darkness.

Paintore through every fibre of my being. The bronze sunlight disappeared, replaced with a dull, overcast gloom reflecting the day outside. The monitor beside me beeped with frantic anxiety, monitoring one of my vital signs. Through the pain I pushed myself into a seated position and looked across to the notebook on my table. A thought struck me. I reached over, and through the gasps

and winces of pain I opened the draw, fumbling around for Chris' ring.
    It had vanished.

Chapter 27: Confronted

"Holy shit," Louis whispered from somewhere beside me. We stopped at the entrance to Moonshine Alley, amazed at the spectacle that stood ahead of us. The clear, moonlit night embraced everything it could find in the world below, ourselves included. The full moon hung high, clear and bright. So bright, in fact, that the craters upon its surface some three hundred and eighty thousand kilometres away stood bold and grey against its glow.

The cloudless sky created a clear path down to the rockface in front of us, and just as the legend foretold, the limestone surface shimmered in a bright, nocturnal light. For a moment you could be forgiven for thinking you had stepped on to an alien planet, one where neon plants and glowing leaves encompassed the vegetation where you walked, but this was not another world. This was Millers Fall, and that glowing surface signified the entrance to our oncoming doom.

"It really does glow," Charlie said, half amazed, half concerned. I'd imagined that on a clear night the rock's surface may have reflected some light, like a basic reflection that could be found on any natural surface, but not like this. Somehow, some way, the moonlight painted the entire wall in a phosphorescent light. Moonshine Alley stood proud within the darkness that otherwise surrounded us.

"This is it," I began, bringing attention back to the task at hand. "Once we step inside..."

I didn't finish my sentence. I didn't want to speak of the possibilities that could overwhelm us.

I expected Louis to make some remark about turning back, going home and hiding under his bed, but he didn't. I felt afraid, of course, but somewhere in my mind a sense of confidence began to emerge. I wondered if Louis felt the same.

Charlie placed out a clenched fist. "For the Wolf Pack."

I fist bumped him. "For the Wolf Pack."

"For the Wolf Pack." Louis leaned in and bumped us.

And for Chris, too.

With nothing more than a flashlight, a penny, a hope and a prayer, we made our way to the darkened trail that stood clear within the glowing rock.

We stepped into the clearing where our lives had all changed. God, it felt like a lifetime ago. The lights we encountered the time before remained, this time glowing shades of blue as they bobbed and danced in an invisible breeze. Like a spiders web caught in the sun, I remembered. But this time the sun had turned blue, and brought about a beautiful colour change that only existed inside this clearing.

Charlie turned the flashlight off. I could see both my friends in a clear, blue light, kind of like those blue night-time shades you see in all those eighties horror movies. The river passed by down in the ravine, unseen but ominously heard. That river had carried the lifeless body of Lonesome Jones down to the lake. A thought struck me as I stood watching the blue lights flickering on and off. If we'd have left Lonesome's body where he fell, would all of this have happened? If we'd have ignored Charlie and just left him there, would we be sat at home right now watching *'Bonanza'* or *'Gunsmoke?'* Hell, I'd even take *'I Dream of Jeanie'* if it meant none of this had ever happened.

Louis lurched to the side and groaned. I fell to the ground, pushed by an unseen force. Charlie stumbled atop my feet and crashed down beside me.

"Well, would you look at what we have here?" came a familiar voice. Troy Peller stepped from the darkness with his side kick Billy Brewster. In the poor light the swelling around Peller's lips and eye stood prominent against his bland features. He swung a baseball bat in his hand, walking around like king shit. Like the alpha male. Louis groaned again and clutched his ribs.

"That was for the fat lip, you little bastard," Peller explained.

"I think you broke something," Louis gasped.

"That ain't all I'm gonna break," king shit replied.

"You bastards!" Charlie stood and charged at them. With his judgement clouded and only able to see red, his focus on Troy allowed Brewster to clock him with a powerful straight, right in the mouth. The impact sent him tumbling down once again.

Peller span the bat in a circle as he wandered around. Brewster did what Brewster always did; watch and laugh.

"What are you shit holes doing out here anyway? So far away from town, and isolated, too. It's one of those places that you could beat the crap out of someone and not be seen," Peller said. "In fact, you could probably kill someone up here and get away with it." He smirked, almost like he knew. That swollen, bruised lip rose a little, and at that moment I knew we were in for a beating. Brewster stepped over and swung his boot into my ribs. My gasp turned to a scream as it lurched from my body into the cold air.

Brewster chuckled. "You boys need to be more careful where you talk. I mean, if you'd have been sat in a diner earlier today, who knows *who* could have overheard your conversation?"

That's when I knew. Unbeknown to us Brewster had entered the diner and overheard what we were saying. Disappointment and pain surged through my being. Disappointment we hadn't kept confidentiality, and pain as another strike smashed into my ribs. This time I cried out.

"Hey Troy. Callum screams like a girl," Brewster stated, pleased as punch that he'd reduced me to tears.

"That's because he's a little bitch."

"You want me to make him do it again?"

"What are you assholes gonna do to us?" Charlie asked, spitting a concoction of saliva and blood on to the grass. Troy stopped and squatted beside him.

"What the fuck do you think I'm going to do, Charlie boy?" He pushed down on the bat and stood upright. The breeze gusted, ruffling my hair as I attempted to sit up. "I'm gonna get my payback. You put me in the hospital, I'm gonna do the same to you." Troy looked to the business end of the bat. "Indefinitely."

"Yeah, well," Charlie began, lifting his broken body up. "Remember one thing, dick head. Everyone saw us beat the shit out of you. Everyone saw you get your ass kicked for the first time ever, by a couple of fourteen year-old kids, and they all laughed and thought it was hilarious. When they wheeled you out of school you were a laughing stock. And guess what? You're the only person on the wrestling team that got beaten up in a dining hall by a group of nerds. You think you're gonna keep that position? That captaincy? Are you fuck."

In the dim light, Troy's face turned from amusement to anger. Charlie was poking the big dog with a stick, and poking him hard. "You know what else? Louis and me are heroes. Actual heroes. In fact, we're so popular that even Erika Ricketts said she'd rather date me than you. She said when push came to shove you just couldn't deliver. Beaten up by a common kid. Face it, Peller. You suck. And when you said to Chris that his dad was ashamed of him, you got it the wrong way around. It's your dad, now. He's ashamed of you. I mean, you even have to attack us with a baseball bat, you can't even do it with your bare hands. Fucking coward."

Troy screamed and swung the weapon toward him. From the darkness a bolt of light thrashed into the bat, shattering it in Peller's hand.

"What the hell?!" he screamed.

Lightning flickered to life within the clearing. It whipped and snapped around us, forming an electrical barrier blocking any escape route.

"I knew you'd come back," a voice echoed from the darkness. Strange, blue flashes exploded within the clearing. Although hurt and barley able to breathe, I managed to sit myself up and watch the oncoming lights as they flashed toward us. Each colour, blue, white and navy became brilliant fluorescent shades, glowing with vibrancy against the darkened area they emerged from. They fused together and took the shape of a man. The man we'd come to banish. Lonesome Jones.

Charlie grimaced. Tears stained Louis' cheeks.

"You alright?" Charlie shouted across, grimacing with every small movement. Peller had really done a number on us.

"I think so," I quivered.

"Good. You're up."

The spirit of Lonesome Jones floated just a few feet away. His skin shone white, and hints of pale but brilliant blue emerged as shadow from his features. A swirling, dancing aura wafted around him, itself a bright combination of both colours. The spirit looked at us, his expression neutral and void.

"Do you wish to die sooner?" he asked, studying us as much as we did him.

"We don't wish to die at all," I answered. My voice exuded confidence instead of fear. I blocked the pain from my ribs. I pushed through the pain barrier and stood up, staring down the spirit levitating ahead of me. I thought I should have been more afraid. We'd been through hell, Charlie, Louis and I, and coming face to face with our tormentor angered me more than anything. Fear had vanished.

"Well, you will," Lonesome snapped, "as punishment for what you did to me."

His voice came from another world. It echoed and warbled in a faint but detectable way. A strange, synthetic tone omitted a second or so before he spoke, giving his vocals a mechanical tinge.

"It was your fault!" Charlie shouted, standing his ground in the face of adversity. "You attacked us! We would have left you alone, and left quietly, but this whole thing was because of you! If you hadn't started the fight we wouldn't have fought back!"

"Hush your mouth." Charlie screamed out. A bolt of light knocked him to the grass.

"Leave us alone!" Louis screamed. "Just leave us alone!"

"Why are you so evil!" I shouted. My emotions bested me. Pain and anger surged from my mouth like hot lava from an exploding volcano. "What made you like this?"

"You did!" Lonesome screamed back. his aura exploded, covering the entire clearing in blinding, white light. "Because of you I walk in purgatory! I cannot cross to the spirit world! You must die! All of you!"

I stood defiant in the brilliant light. My anger didn't quell. I ached. I hurt, but still I stood tall. Fumbling in my pocket I found the penny and lifted it into the light.

"This is not the place for you! Now is your time to leave! Go away! Go away and leave us alone!"

Charlie's voice emerged from the light. "Fuck you, asshole. Get the fuck away from us!"

"Go away!" came Louis defiant voice.

We shouted. We screamed. We let the whole world know we wouldn't be afraid any more.

"Go away!"
"Leave!"
"Go!"
"It's not your place!"
"Go way!"
"leave us alone!"
"Go away!"
"Go away!"
"GO AWAY!"

I slumped to the grass. Confused for a moment I shook my head, attempting to remove the cobwebs that had taken residence inside. The sodden ground chilled my body as I lay upon its surface, my clothes all but saturated through. The throbbing, blunt pain omitting from my side didn't let up. It pounded like a battering ram against a castle door that needed to be breached. The injuries I sustained during Peller's attack hurt like hell. I'd need medical attention, that was for sure.

Just across from me Louis sat upright. Charlie winced as he moved from his prone position.

"Louis, what happened?" I croaked, pushing myself up once again.

"He's gone."

I shook my head once more and attempted to gain my bearings. The river crashed past, that much I could hear. The darkness had returned. I reached over and took Charlie's flashlight in my hand, all whilst fighting the pain surging through my body. With limited movement I scoured every nook with the tell-tale-light and found nothing. We'd been left alone.

"Is that it?" Charlie asked. He sounded and looked beaten. How he'd explain this to his parents when he got home I had no idea. But then, how were Louis and I going to explain it? We were beaten up, covered in mud and soaked to the core. This would be a grounding for a month, if not longer.

"I think so," I began, bringing my attention back to the here and now. The atmosphere that hung heavy just a moment ago had all but lifted.

Roots exploded from the ground, encircling me within a tight, constricted grip. The smell of damp earth filled my nose as they immobilised my body, showering me with clumps of mud with each attack. A light emerged ahead, and from it the spirit of Lonesome Jones drifted into view.

I lost hope. Unable to move, unable to scream, I knew then my time had come. Lonesome would not wait any longer in purgatory. The promise of killing us one by one had disintegrated. The spirit scowled as he approached.

"Now you die..."

Charlie and Louis gasped and grunted, no doubt caught up in the living foliage. We could not escape. We were done for…

Miss Wincott appeared in my mind. She sat at her table the same as when I interviewed her, but this time she appeared serious. I recalled something from that conversation. Gabriel? Guardian angels…

"Remember, Callum… Just ask… Close your eyes and speak to them. Reach out. Ask for help."

"Please… please hear me," I began in prayer. "Archangel Gabriel, any angel, please help me. Please… help us."

I opened my eyes. Lonesome's face contorted into a vile, twisted grin. I groaned as the restrictions drew tighter.

"Please hear me... please... help..."

Lightning thrashed into the clearing, destroying my binds and eviscerating the ground. Mud, earth and grass seared into the air. Bright light burned throughout the clearing. I pulled myself free of the dying roots and shaded my eyes. Lonesome

Jones screamed a long, sorrowful, synthetic scream. His features faded as he thrashed around. They peeled away to reveal the skull behind them. His spirit crumbled and wafted upwards in brilliant, blue embers.

The light faded. The sound of the river came easing back. The isolated area returned to its usual, tranquil self, except of course for the cratered ground where the lightning had struck.

A cough emerged from beside me. Louis wiped his face and spat on to the ground. Charlie ruffled his hair. Mud tumbled out. I realised my own hair had been covered, and I too wiped away the earth that landed on me.

"What was that?" Louis asked, shaking his arms to remove any rogue pieces he'd missed.

"I don't know," Charlie began, mirroring Louis' movements, "but it looks like the hobo motherfucker didn't stick around to find out."

"He got burnt," I said, explaining what I'd seen inside the light.

Charlie frowned. "What do you mean?"

"Not like burnt with fire. It was like the light. It burned him away. didn't you guys see it?"

They shook their heads.

"I couldn't see anything in that," Louis replied.

"Speaking of that light, where the hell did it come from? Was it lightning?"

Charlie asked a valid question. Above us, through the tree tops, stars twinkled in the cold night sky. Not even a hint of a cloud passed over head. I didn't see how lightning could exist with the absence of storm clouds.

Across the crater a light began to flicker. It flashed and danced much like the ones we'd witnessed before, only this time it grew in stature. An aura emerged. Inside, the silhouette of a person took shape, and that person walked toward us. I dropped my head and sighed. Whatever we did to rid ourselves of the spirit just didn't seem to work. At that moment, the fight I'd had inside vanished into the ether. I couldn't go on any longer. I'd built a barrier around me, keeping fate on the outside for as long as I could. Despite my best efforts, that barrier had crumbled, and I had nothing left to rebuild it with.

I accepted whatever the future held for me.

"Holy shit," Louis gasped in amazement. "Look. Look!"

The shadow moved closer, and with each step became less and less hidden. It emerged, revealing itself in all its brilliant glory.

"I don't believe it," I whispered, unable to process what I saw.

Within the bright aura a spirit did stand. However, it was not the reviled spirit of Lonesome Jones like I thought. A slim, smaller person emerged from the light, harbouring a huge, amused smile.

"Hey douchbags. Never forget that I was your guardian angel."

I took a few steps toward the spirit. "Is it really you? Is it really, really you?"

Indeed it was. Our guardian angel had been none other than Chris Lester himself.

"This is so trippy," Charlie said. Both he and Louis looked on in amazement.

"I thought you were dead?" Louis asked. You could always count on him to bring us back to down to earth.

"I am," Chris replied. He too spoke with that strange, synthetic sound that had also tainted Lonesome Jones' voice.

"Chris..." I began, attempting to find logic in the situation. "What's happened? What are you doing here? where's Lonesome Jones?"

"You don't need to worry about him. He's passed to where he belongs. He's not gonna haunt you any longer."

"What did you do to him?" Charlie asked.

"My light burnt the resentment from him. He was able to be at peace."

"You have a special kind of light?" I asked, still not sure if I followed the explanation fully.

"Only in this situation. I'm your guardian. I can protect you from threats, but only if they're spiritual. Anything else and you're on your own."

I stood in awe, studying my friend's spirit. He appeared more vivid than the one who attempted to collect our souls. I guessed this was a reflection of the person he was in life. A friend. A true friend.

Chris' expression changed, and his smile became one of love.

"I gotta go, guys. We don't get much time down here."

"Wait!" Louis snapped, drawing Chris' attention. "Are you okay? Are you happy?"

Chris nodded. "I am. Everything just seems to have lifted. I'm not troubled any more. There's no worry. Well, there's nothing to even worry about. I can't explain it. You'll see what I mean one day."

"Chris?" Charlie quipped, eager to ask one final question. "What's it like dying?"

"It's nothing you should worry about, Charlie. Don't ever fear it, okay?"

Charlie nodded.

Embers emerged from his body, like florescent blue fireflies floating into the sky. His body broke down into thousands of shards, all glowing, all ascending to the heavens.

"Bye guys," he said, holding up a hand that dispersed into the air.

We watched as he vanished in a plethora of light, ascending up into the trees and then the night sky.

He disappeared as gracefully as he arrived.

Chapter 28: Aftermath

Coming back down to earth after this whole ordeal was a lot more painful, both physical and emotional. The beating I'd received from Billy Brewster reminded me that pain existed, and would do for quite some time. My entire body hurt, and I found myself shambling instead of walking.

"Hey," I said, remembering our tormentors. "What the hell happened to Peller and Brewster?"

We scanned the clearing with our flashlights, wincing in pain and moaning about the beating we had taken. We found them, nursing some minor ailments they'd sustained somehow. As we approached, Peller stood up like an old man, all shaky and uncontrollable. He held his palms out.

"I'm sorry, okay? I'm sorry. Please?"

A smile crossed my face. I'd never heard of an older kid being afraid of someone younger than himself, but here we were. I looked back at my friends.

"Let's go home."

We left Moonshine Alley together. All of us. Peller and Brewster included. As soon as we stepped from the trail back into the woodland we swore to never go back there again.

And we never did.

Chapter 29: The Years After

So, Aunt Penny finally got her divorce signed and sealed. She continued her work in Millers Fall until one day she pulled a guy over for speeding. Turns out she went on a date with him and subsequently married the guy. She moved out to Florida and became a stay-at-home mom, raising two boys down there in the sunshine state. She lived out her life without a single health problem, dying peacefully at home aged eighty-two. You live the life your dealt with, and boy did she have a good one.

    Ted continued working for a few years, and I continued my Saturday job alongside him for a short while after. In 1975 a business man blew through town and offered him a substantial amount to purchase the business. Ted, being of a certain age, took the money and ran, as anyone in his position would do. One day out of the blue he turned up on my doorstep and slipped me one hundred bucks of the sale money, saying I'd earned it as much as he had. That set me up good. Last I heard he was travelling Europe. He'll never know how much he helped me.

    Chris' mom wasn't so much of a happy ending. After Chris she lost everything, not just her property. She found herself committed to a hospital in an attempt to get her back on track again. I don't think they ever did. That's all I heard. Chris' dad never returned home. He was officially declared missing in '70, but by then his mom had already lost her shit. I don't know what became of her.

My Mom and Dad continued as normal, until the late nineties when Dad became ill. He was diagnosed with dementia, and as the years passed he became a huge burden on my Mom. He lost a little piece of himself every day, until he no longer knew her, me or what he did. The final straw came when he beat my Mom up. As much as we hated it, we had him placed into the system. Mom couldn't cope with his behaviour, and I couldn't justify him staying at home beating the hell out of her.

About three months after this happened she passed away. To this day I believe she died of a broken heart. Dad passed away in care a few years later. Even though it was a terrible period in my life, I always thought back to the Lonesome Jones saga and remembered just how bad that had been. I think it desensitised me to emotional situations, allowing me to deal with them in an efficient manner.

Now, in order for you to know about Sheriff Lewis I have to tell you something else first. Stacey Shawcross and I ended up getting married, believe it or not. Erika was telling the truth. Although it hasn't been plain sailing, we've remained married all these years.

It must have been around '76, something like that when I bumped into, well, Mr Lewis as he was known then, after retiring. Stacey and I had arranged to meet at the bar one Friday evening when she finished work. I arrived on time, but then took a phone call from the barman that said she'd be running late. As I sat there cradling a beer Mr Lewis walked in, looking relaxed, content, and free of the stresses of police work. I brought him a beer and he perched on the stool beside me. We chatted for what felt like an age, and something came up that I least expected.

"You remember the whole Lonesome Jones escapade that happened a few years back?" he asked, almost causing me to spill my drink.

"Yeah? Died up in the woods if I remember correctly?"

Lewis nodded. "Yes, that's right."

"Didn't you tell me the case was closed?"

"It was when I left. Never found anything to re-open it."

I took a swig of my beer, trying to think of a subject to divert the conversation.

"You know what really gets me?" he said, lowering his voice and leaning closer. "*You* knew how he was killed before the information was released. You remember?"

"I also remember telling you it was a thought, and that most people suffer head injuries or sprains up in those woods."

Lewis' demeanour changed. "Don't bullshit me, Callum. I know you were involved. I know that your fingerprints are on this somewhere. You don't realise just how lucky you were. The coroner ruled it accidental, even though questions were raised about the head injury Lonesome Jones sustained. If he'd have determined any other cause of death I'd have hauled your ass in on the grounds that you knew all about the injury before it became public knowledge. You were one lucky bastard that day. I couldn't connect you to it any other way, that's why you walked free." He slammed his empty bottle on the bar and slapped me on the back. "Great catching up with you, Callum. I'll see you around."

But he never did. That was the last time we laid eyes upon each other, and to say I was thankful was an understatement.

Troy Peller and Billy Brewster took a relaxed stance with us from there on in. Not once did they seek any of us out to ask what had happened up there in Moonshine Alley. They continued on as though nothing had happened, and left us alone for the rest of their school years. Billy Brewster's folks moved out of state once he finished his education, and no one heard anything of him afterwards. Troy went off to college on a scholarship, making it his life goal to compete at wrestling in the Olympic Games. I always kept an eye out for him during the event, but it seems he never made it. Last I heard, he was selling used cars to pay his bills.

Charlie became more serious. Yes, he still goofed around but not to the extent he had before our run in with Lonesome Jones. He didn't argue with the teachers, he didn't make an ass of himself and he stopped harassing Erika Ricketts. A week or so after our last visit to the clearing, both he and Louis were reinstated to school, and the first thing he did was apologise to her. She took it with grace, and as the weeks wore on they said hello in passing.

Remember the boyfriend from out of town? The one they all thought belonged to a motorcycle gang? Well, it turns out he had a long-term lover back in the town he hailed from. Of course, when Erika found this out she dumped him quicker than a hiccup, and spent until early 1970 on the market. And you know what I'm going to say, right? Charlie invited her to the school valentine disco of that year. She accepted, and the rest was history. Charlie, that son of a bitch. That god *damned* son of a bitch.

They were good together and she introduced him to her passion for drama and acting. Now, Charlie would tell you different. He'd tell you that he always loved acting and wanted to be an actor, ever since he was a kid. We all knew it was bullshit and just a way to spend more time with Erika. But, it was something he became good at. He appeared in school productions, and later on in plays that he worked on during college. Yes, Charlie went to acting college. With Erika, of course. But that wasn't his main reason for going. He went purely to study theatrics, and not at all because Erika went there. He thought we were born yesterday. Idiot.

As the seventies blew past he built up his resume, and by 1981 secured his first big role on Broadway, appearing in '*Frankenstein*,' alongside the delectable Diane Wiest. However, this didn't last long and his role was recast after his agent (yes, Charlie had a talent agent) secured him a role on the daytime television show '*Fields of Cane*,' in which he played Chris (coincidence or what) Temple, a farmhand who oversaw the slaves on a plantation.

As the years passed, Louis and I made the effort to attend the opening night on his productions, cheering him on as he brought various characters to life. And much like his fourteen year-old self, he loved every single moment of it. Charlie always strived to be better, and for whatever reason he could not make the jump to the mainstream. This brought about a descent into depression. He argued, he shouted, he became miserable, but through it all Erika stuck with him. That changed, though, when she discovered him abusing drugs and alcohol. He swore it was a coping mechanism, but it didn't convince her.

She left him not long after, and it broke his heart. He dived head first into constant drug use, and no matter what Louis or I did to help, he couldn't overcome his addiction. One morning in April 1988 he'd failed to show for the rehearsal of a play he was appearing in. A welfare check was called in, and staff at his hotel forced entry into his room. Charlie laid curled in the foetal position with a needle protruding from his arm. He died of an overdose, succumbing to his demons like so many in that industry. The acting business creates so much stress for so many people, that overdoses seem to be considered normal amongst them these days. Charlie left us aged 34.

Louis experienced a somewhat traditional start to life after school. He found work at the local lumber mill just outside Millers Fall, married a girl named Dotty and rose two children. The heavy work he'd taken on took its toll, and by his early thirties he'd started work as a care provider in a psychiatric institute a few miles south of town. He stuck this job for the rest of his life, but he hated every second of it.

When we met up, he'd always complain about the abuse he'd been subjected to from the patients, and the wild things he'd seen in the way of treatment. He'd been beaten up, cut, spat on, you name it, he'd suffered, and the thought of having to work that job sent him spiralling. Things picked up as the years rolled on. His working environment became somewhat safer, but Louis got stuck with the care card. No matter what job he applied for, he was rejected. On February 6th 2000, his wife, Dotty, contacted the police after he failed to return home from work. A check with his employer showed he didn't clock in that day.

A search was launched a day later, and a few hours in they found him. He sat up against a tree in the surrounding woodland. Brain matter, bone and blood scattered the surrounding area. He'd taken a shotgun, downed a crate of beer and blown his own head off. Of course, his family were devastated. A suicide note found in his pocket explained why. He'd been fed up and angry with the world. There didn't appear to be any way out for him. Stuck in a job he hated, for a minimal wage, with $7,000 worth of debt on his shoulders he had no way of paying back. He did the only thing he thought he could. And you know what? I hated him for it. As much as I loved him, I hated him for leaving me on my own.

Me? Well, not much happened that you don't already know. Stacey and I married once our daughter arrived. Things were good for the best part, but the development of an illness in my mid-fifties laid to rest the plans I had in my advancing years. From that moment on I spent most of my time in and out of hospital, lounging at home and being a burden on my family.

In a strange way, I look back on things now and think Lonesome Jones succeeded in what he set out to achieve. He didn't kill us all like he intended that night up in Moonshine Alley, but looking at the lives we had since makes me believe that he got exactly what he wanted. All of my friends killed themselves. They all fell into a depression that caused them to take their own lives. They were all unhappy leading up to the event. The only exception was me, but then again, I've been living with illness for longer than I'd like to remember.

Now it looks like my time is up. Chris, Charlie and Louis are loitering around, poking their heads out of the shadows, waiting for me to finish this confession. I know that this will start a new investigation. I know that my name will be scrutinized and investigated. I know I'm going to bring some distress to my family and everyone involved. I've kept this secret for nearly 44 years, and I needed to write it down and release the weight from my shoulders. Whatever happens from here on is out of my hands. I've confessed. People will know the truth.

The more I think about it, the more it makes sense. We cleansed ourselves of the haunting, but we didn't cleanse ourselves of the curse.

That old bastard got us good.